CRAIG A. PRICE
SHAYNE PRICE

SPACE CATS
MAKING ENEMIES

contents

space cats:

Making Enemies

Space Cats
Book One

craig a. price

shayne a. price

paws and reflect

. . .

Blake

To boldly go where no cat has gone before!

Blake's brown tail waved back and forth as he paced on the bridge aboard his ship, the StormCat. The shutters on the window opened wide, causing starlight to flood the room, and the haunting beauty of the deep purple planet they approached illuminated the darkness. Inside the bridge, the cats worked tirelessly, constantly working the controls, and would often take naps if they weren't doing anything. It was way more efficient than the way of humans, who were always constantly without rest.

The CEC, or Cat Exploration Corporation, demanded felines explore any solar system they passed, searching for intelligent life out there. More intelligent than the humans they'd left behind on earth. After all, humans were nothing but savages who spent all day worrying and working rather than doing something productive… like napping or chasing mice.

Blake's eyes grew drowsy as he thought about sleep. He ceased pacing, curled up and laid down on the floor, feeling the cold metal under his belly, and purred.

"Captain, we're here," Azalea said, turning from her chair.

Blake stretched, his paws trembling as he nearly hissed at Azalea for disturbing his nap. But he could not hold her to blame. This was what they were tasked with doing.

Once they finished with this system, Blake could get his much deserved nap before they arrived at the next location. Licking his chomps, he sauntered over to Azalea, standing to his hind legs and peering at the screen. "Have you run the scanners?"

"Searching for life now, Captain." Azalea looked back to her second monitor, where she pawed at a mouse behind the screen.

The system beeped and Azalea turned from her game to look at the screen once more. "Scans for life have come back negative, sir. The atmosphere is not breathable."

"Right." Blake ran his paw through his matted fur, then turned around to stroll back to his chair, his tail flicking in the air. "Ready the engines. It's time to head to the next system, and take a much needed nap."

"Sir?" Fransis interjected.

Blake turned to the scientist. Fransis was the most curious cat Blake knew. One day, it was going to get him killed. "What is it, Fransis?"

"I would like to explore the planet."

"For what?" Blake hissed. "We've already determined there is no life on it. And we can't breathe on the surface. What would you have us do?"

"I want to collect samples."

"Don't you have enough samples in your lab?" Blake yawned.

"Please?" Fransis asked. "I just want a sample of some of that purple gas."

"What for?" Blake asked.

"I've been running experiments with catnip with various gas and vapors, and would love to see how this gas reacts with it."

Blake twirled his paw in his whiskers. "Fine… but don't waste all the catnip. Set a course for the planet's surface."

Blake motioned for Fransis and Azalea to follow him. A few other cats moved from their positions on the bridge to fill the gaps they left as the three of them went to the decompression chamber.

He knew he shouldn't be traveling to the planet with

the others. After all, he was the captain. His place was on the bridge. He had people to send out to the planet, and for a moment, he thought about it. But that wasn't why he got into this business. Blake was an explorer at heart. He wanted to see the stars. To go where no cat had gone before. He wanted to make his family proud.

Blake had never met his father. His mother told him he was a farmer. Blake wished he had known him. He spent many catnaps wondering what his father was like. All he knew was that his father magically disappeared when he was still an infant. He liked to imagine the amazing catnip his father grew and hoped he could make him proud by being on the go as an adventurer—an adventurer like him. At least, that was what Blake hoped had happened to his father. Surely he hadn't just abandoned him. No, that wasn't what he dreamed about. His father was out there somewhere, on some grand adventure. And Blake would make him proud. He was no scaredy cat. Blake had to fulfill his dreams, no matter the costs.

They all put on their space suits and waited for the red light to turn green. It only took a few more minutes for the light to turn when the ship jerked slightly as it touched down on the surface.

Blake was the first one to step out of the ship and glance around. He observed the planet seemed to be mostly made up of gas, but upon looking closer, he saw a few strange objects buzzing around him. Were they life?

They reminded him of insects, particularly the flies he used to chase while still a kitten back on earth.

Fransis got straight to work, using jars to catch the purple vapors. He even captured a few of the strange objects floating around in separate glass containers. Blake and the others who had joined monitored the perimeter to ensure nothing strange had occurred. They were prepared, blasters at the ready—just in case.

Once Fransis finished his samples, they went back to the StormCat. All of them were tired, and quite ready for a nap. Fransis departed the shuttle bay immediately and left for the Research Laboratory.

When Blake stepped back onto the bridge, he discovered everyone was asleep. A light, muffled purring lingered in the otherwise silent room. Each purr complimented another in a beautiful harmony.

Blake's nose twitched, and he meowed.

Everyone stretched to attention.

"Did everyone get a good nap?" Blake asked.

"I did," Azalea purred.

"Rhetorical. We've talked about this. You cannot all nap at the same time. What if we're attacked?"

"We would have sensed an attack," Azalea said. "Besides… we have nine lives."

"Now you know that's not true. That was used to make us cats more superior," Blake said sarcastically.

Azalea frowned. "Yeah, but no one has to know, now do they?"

"Let's get out of this system so we can properly take a nap."

"Aye, Captain."

The ship shook as they headed out of the system. Blake stretched his paw and clawed at his chair to prevent the ship from tossing him across the bridge. Others weren't as lucky. Diego hung onto his chair with his claws as long as he could before letting loose and flying across the room, hitting the wall; but of course, he landed on his feet.

"What was that?" Blake asked.

"We're nearing a volcanic planet," Azalea said unsteadily as she clawed herself to a chair, watching the monitors.

"We're in space. How is that affecting us?"

"The pressure of the planet's volcanoes is excessive. It's blowing out volcanic rock into the atmosphere, and shards of it are slamming against the exterior hull."

"Is it dangerous?"

"I don't know how much more our hull can take before a shard penetrates it."

Blake growled. He glanced side to side, trying to find where the pilot had gone, before he remembered he was the pilot. He pounced into the air for the steering column. Slamming the controls to the left, he maneuvered the ship away from the erupting volcanos of the planet, and into empty space. A few more pieces of space debris collided with the hull before they were out of the volcanic storm.

They were clear as Blake hit the controls to make the jump to the next system. It had been quite a day, and now it was time for a nap. He yawned, curled up on his captain's chair, and began snoozing.

flyball and furious

. . .

Shadow

In space, no one can resist the charm of a wagging tail.

Shadow meticulously organized his den, ensuring that every item was in its proper place. A dog had to keep his den nice. While Shadow worked on organizing his things, his mentor, Obsidian, walked into the den. Shadow was under Obsidian as an apprentice. He looked up to Obsidian. They often worked together on various tasks and missions.

Obsidian noticed Shadow's attention to detail. "Are you preparing for an inspection?"

Shadow nodded, his paw resting on some of his

paperwork. "I don't want to be caught with my tongue hanging out of my mouth."

Obsidian, understanding his apprentice's dedication, offered to help him finish up the organization. Eight paws were better than four. Together, they worked to make sure the den was spotless and ready for any potential inspection.

"I believe that is clean enough, Shadow. It's time for morning training," Obsidian said.

Shadow nodded, and they began their routine training. When it came to catching tennis balls, Shadow was a pro, and tackling Obsidian with the football was not much of a challenge either. Shadow loved to do it all, especially when he had an excellent mentor who did a great job of helping him. Even though Obsidian was kind of independent and strict, he was a good teacher. If there was one thing Shadow did not like, it was being all by himself.

Obsidian was always a paw behind Shadow with football. Football was not really Obsidian's thing. He'd rather be doing secret covert missions for the Dog Empire, but he was stuck with having to train Shadow to prove his worth. Shadow was the dog's bark when it came to football. It was his favorite sport. Nobody could ever get the ball from him when he had it, especially when he stayed in shape. Obsidian could be grumpy at times, especially whenever he lost to Shadow all the time.

As they were training, Max, one of Geoff's assistants, came running into the training room, his paws pattering against the cold steel floors. He came to a thudding stop and panted. "Geoff needs to see you both in his quarters right away."

Shadow and Obsidian exchanged a worried glance before following Max to Geoff's quarters through the winding corridors. It was hard keeping up with Max, as he was fast. He had to be as an assistant to Geoff. Shadow did well keeping up, as he was young and in shape, but Obsidian trailed a little behind.

It didn't take long to reach Geoff's quarters. Shadow paused outside of the door as Max rushed in. He turned around and saw Obsidian panting a dozen yards behind. Shadow was a good dog, as he sat and waited for his master. Once they were reunited, Obsidian nodded to Shadow and the two of them stepped inside of the office.

"I have a very important mission for the two of you." Geoff paced back and forth when they walked in. "It's a matter of great urgency, and I need you to begin it as soon as possible."

"Of course, Geoff. What's the mission?" Obsidian asked, his tail wagging. "It's about time I break free from here and embrace the celestial world outside."

Shadow knew Obsidian was finally ready to get out of this boring place.

Geoff paused, looking at them both. "I'm afraid I can't

go into too much detail just yet, but I will tell you it involves a graduation and a final test for your training, Shadow. I hope that Obsidian has trained you well because it will be a tough challenge."

Shadow's heart sank. He had been working with his fellow trainees for months, and the graduation ceremony was meant to be the proudest moment of his career. Shadow had been looking forward to it for so long, but he didn't expect it so soon. He wasn't sure if he was a hundred percent ready yet. "I understand, Geoff." Shadow gulped. "I will do whatever it takes to complete the mission."

Geoff nodded, looking pleased. "Good. The final test will be a hard challenge, but I know you're up for it. There are three parts to it. The first is a fighting challenge, where you must show your skills in the ring. Second is a flying challenge, where you must fly a spaceship and destroy targets in a certain amount of time. The last and third challenge is a game of capture the flag. You must retrieve a desired item, getting past security and not getting caught."

Shadow and Obsidian looked at each other. Shadow knew that this was going to be a hard challenge, but he was determined to succeed.

"When is the test?" Shadow asked.

"Right now."

"Now?" Obsidian barked. "We don't get any time to train for it?"

Geoff laughed. "What do you think you've been doing all this time? You've been training every single day. I've kept tabs on you and Shadow. You are the best we've got. You never stop training. This should be a walk in the park."

Shadow took a deep breath, hiding his tongue back in his mouth. "I'm ready."

Geoff led them to the testing arena. It wasn't crowded, but there were a handful of spectators. Other dogs who would assess them based on their scores. He hoped his recruits would be up for the test, but he too needed to prove himself. He needed to show he was capable of being a leader. It was time to no longer be considered a puppy. It was time to be a dog.

Shadow entered the ring. He didn't care for fighting, but he knew it was all part of his training. It was all to prepare him for a mission. Shadow couldn't be afraid. They depended on him. The dog who faced him had drool foaming at the mouth. This would not be easy.

"Come on," Shadow growled. "Throw a dog a bone."

His opponent charged at him, but Shadow dove to the side, nipping at the other dog's ankles. The two circled around each other, trying to gain an advantage, but the other dog was much stronger. Shadow couldn't use his strength to be victorious. He would have to use his smarts.

He calculated his moves. Each nip and swipe precise. They fought fiercely and unyieldingly. He yipped when the other dog got his tail, and Shadow nearly put his tail between his legs and trotted off, but people depended on him. He couldn't give up now. Shadow growled back, leaping forward and bringing the other dog to the ground, biting at his neck.

He brought the dog down but not long enough. The dog then shook Shadow off and growled fiercely. Shadow knew this was going to be a tough fight and knew the only way to defeat the stronger dog was to tire him. Shadow ran around the ring in circles and made the other dog dizzy. He then jumped to the top of the ring and pounced on the dog, who was too tired and dizzy to shake him off this time.

The bell rang.

Shadow was victorious.

Next, he needed to prove himself as the best pilot.

Shadow sat in the spaceship's cockpit, his hands gripping the controls tightly. Filled with nerves, he contemplated backing down, but his loyalty as a dog prevented him from doing so. The ship was a sleek, black vessel that had been designed for speed and agility. They equipped it with state-of-the-art weapons and shields that would protect Shadow from any attacks. He was nervous since he never flew a real ship, just a simulation when he was training.

He activated the ship's engines and began his routine. He started off by warming up the engines, adjusting the thrusters, and checking all the systems. Once he was sure everything was in good working order, he began his training.

Shadow set the ship to flight simulation mode and began practicing his maneuvers. He flew through tight spaces, dodging and weaving through obstacles. He practiced his aim and shot at targets, honing his skills. As he flew through the vast expanse of space, Shadow felt a rush of adrenaline coursing through his veins. He was in his element, and he loved the thrill of flying.

While he trained, Shadow's mind was laser focused, and he was in complete control of the ship. He knew that this was his chance to prove himself as one of the best pilots in the galaxy.

Suddenly, the ship's alarm went off. Shadow's heart skipped a beat as he saw a fleet of enemy ships approaching fast. He wondered if this was a simulation, or if this was the real deal. He quickly activated the ship's weapons systems, undocked it from simulation mode, and prepared for battle.

Shadow flew the ship in circles, dodging the blaster fire from the enemy ships. He returned fire. Careful to avoid all the attacks, he maneuvered his ship with barrel rolls, shifts to port and starboard, and several other evasive maneuvers. He loved flying in space. It was much more flexible compared to flying on a planet. There was no up or down. Instead, he could move himself around in any position.

A laser struck his rear deflectors, and for a moment he believed he was in real trouble. Checking his rear cameras, he saw three enemy ships closing fast. He pulled his controls hard left, causing his ship to spin port. Shadow then pulled his steering right, causing port rotation as the ship flew starboard. A few more strikes on his rear deflectors, then silence. He turned all engines off, pulled his steering hard, causing his ship to flip a hundred and eighty degrees. The three ships came straight for him, but now, he had a clear shot.

Shadow grinned as he pulled the trigger. One. Two. Three.

With the last ship destroyed, Shadow let out a victorious cry. He had saved the day and had proven himself to be one of the best pilots in the galaxy. He flew the ship back to the base, where everyone greeted him as the champion and praised for his skills.

His victory was short-lived, as it was time for his last test. He met back up with Obsidian, and they were on the same team together. Shadow much preferred team exercises compared to solo missions, and he was grateful they allowed his mentor to do this exercise with him. He was ready for capture the flag. The team who successfully stole and returned the flag first would be triumphant.

Shadow and Obsidian moved swiftly through the dark corridors of the enemy base. They had just finished their last training exercise and were now ready to put their skills to the test. Their objective was to infiltrate the enemy base, where the flag was being held, and retrieve it without getting caught. They needed to be careful not to encounter other teams.

They crept through the shadows, staying out of the sight of the enemy guards. Obsidian had studied the layout of the base and knew where the flag was being held. They had to be careful not to set off any alarms or trip any motion sensors.

As they made their way deeper into the base, they encountered a few guards. Shadow used his stealthiness to take them down quietly, one by one, alerting none of the others. Meanwhile, Obsidian used his knowledge of the base to guide them through the maze of corridors and rooms.

Finally, they reached the room where the flag was being held. The room where the flag was being held had heavy security, but Shadow and Obsidian had a plan. They split up, with Shadow taking out the guards on the left, while Obsidian took out the guards on the right. With the guards taken care of, they quickly retrieved the flag and made their way back to the exit.

As they almost made it to the exit, another dog and his mentor stood in the way. The dog growled. "Hand us the flag, and we won't hurt you. "

"No way." Shadow stood his ground.

Obsidian attacked the other mentor while Shadow tried to get past the other dog. The other dog was much bigger than Shadow and blocked the exit. He grabbed Shadow by the neck and tossed him aside. Shadow regained his footing and noticed a gap under the dog's leg. He swiftly slipped underneath and made his way toward the exit.

As they emerged from the base, everyone greeted them with cheers and applause. They had successfully completed their mission and retrieved the flag without being caught. Shadow had proven himself to be a formidable teammate and was ready for whatever challenges lay ahead.

planet pawscovery

. . .

Jade

Space is full of mysteries, just like an unopened cardboard box!

Jade and his team, including Ryan, Autumn, and Jasper, were tasked with collecting metals and minerals from various planets for the Mineral Mining Corporation. They had explored long and hard, searching for anything that would be of use for the MMC, when their radar caught something they didn't expect.

Inbetween solar systems, they had a blip on their radar. Normally, they would just ignore it and go about their day. In space, there were all kinds of rogue objects in the middle of the vastness of space. Asteroids, space debris, old destroyed spaceships from when humans thought they were smarter than cats and went to explore the galaxy. However, this was different. It was larger. Much larger.

They approached the anomaly on their radar, and Jade was astonished to see a massive orange planet stranded in the middle of nowhere. It wasn't moving, but just suspended there without rotation or movement.

"Jasper, are you seeing this?" Jade asked, his bright green eyes glimmering as he watched the viewscreen.

"Yeah, do you think a giant cat chased it all the way out here?"

"Can you get any readings on the rogue planet? What is keeping it here? Is there any gravitational pull taking it further into space?"

Jasper scratched his bare back. He really needed to put some fur on, except for the fact his breed didn't have fur. Perhaps he needed a jacket to stay warm. Besides, he may look cool with a jacket. "I'm not seeing anything, boss."

"Nothing has a lock on this planet?" Jade flicked his whiskers.

"Nope. It seems to be forgotten about."

Jade purred. "Scan the surface. Perhaps we can find trace minerals here to bring back to the MMC."

Jasper worked on his scanner, sitting at his console. He yawned. He really needed a nap, but his boss was depending on him. The readings were irregular, which had Jasper sitting at the front of his seat.

"What is it?" Jade asked.

"I'm reading a lot of minerals on this planet, but several aren't showing up in our database."

Jade meowed. "Explain."

"I can get some of the bio-composition of the trace minerals, but the overall substance is foreign to what they cataloged in the MMC."

"How is that possible? MMC has been cataloging minerals for generations. Not to mention all the catalogs we've stolen from the humans as well."

"I don't know. I can't explain it." Jasper licked his chomps. "I can't even comprehend it. The only way we'll be able to find out anything is if we explore it ourselves."

"Explore?" Ryan beamed.

"Hold on, Ryan," Jade cautioned.

"The possibilities are endless. We can bring a new mineral to the MMC. We'll be hailed as heroes." Ryan meowed. "They'll give us so much catnip."

"Hold on, Ryan," Jade said again. "Remember what they say about curiosity?"

"Come on, Jade. Cats are explorers. We're catsplorers. This is what we're meant to be doing." Ryan pranced to the window to get a better look at the glowing orange planet.

"We can't just prance in."

"Why not?" Ryan moaned.

"It could be dangerous," Jade said.

"Oh, come on. It'll be fine."

"Hold on, let me talk to command," Jade reminded him.

"Fine, but hurry up. This is our chance to shine." Ryan frowned.

"Whatever." Jade turned away from Ryan. "Jasper, connect me to the MMC."

"Yes, boss," Jasper said.

After a few minutes, the director of the MMC answered the call, and his face appeared on the bridge's viewscreen. "Yes, Jade?"

"Director, we've found a rogue planet between systems we were exploring. On the planet, our scans show there are many trace minerals, including a rich source of an unknown mineral."

"Unknown mineral?" the director asked.

"Yes," Jade responded. "Ryan says it's nowhere in the MMC database."

The director purred.

"How should we proceed?"

"Collect samples. Be cautious."

"Yes, sir."

The screen went black.

"We get to go exploring," Ryan purred.

Jade shook his head. "We still need to be cautious."

"Whatever."

Autumn decided to stay on the ship for an emergency, while Jade, Jasper, and Ryan prepared for their journey. Jade really wanted to get this over with so he could take a nap. He'd been awake for nearly forty-five minutes now, and he was feeling tired. Jade wondered if he could take a short catnap before they got started, but he knew they had to continuously update the MMC since they were on watch protocol while investigating the strange planet.

They set up all the security protocols, including their transporting beams on red alert to pull them from the surface of the planet should anything go awry. They also had several emergency protocols to put into place, and Jade sent out the probes to the planet's surface to test its atmosphere.

Being a cat wasn't easy, and being a part of the MMC even more so. They were expected to do the unexpected. They didn't always get the naps they wanted, but it was all part of the job. It had its benefits. There was a mouse chasing exercising program. Catnip for a job well done. Complimentary balls of yarn. And all you could eat lettuce. It wasn't an awful life. But sometimes, it was exhausting. They were always exhausted.

They entered the decompression chamber and prepared themselves to go to the planet. The readings had come back, showing it has a hospitable atmosphere with enough oxygen to breathe. However, Jade was always cautious. Cats didn't have nine lives like in the stories. He didn't want any cat to fall on his watch.

Jade, Ryan, and Jasper suited up, securing their space-suits and prepared to step on the planet. Jade was nervous, though that was always how he felt. He was the leader for a reason. If they had put Ryan in charge, they'd all have lost their lives by now. Jade was cautious. Nervous. He was careful. Jade wanted them all to come home safely. He took a deep breath, then looked at the others.

"Is everyone ready?"

"Ready, boss," Jasper said.

"Do you think there are any mice on this planet?" Ryan asked.

Jade ignored him. "Let's do this."

cat-astrophic encounter

. . .

Shadow

Space exploration is a walk in the park... a really, really big park!

Shadow and Obsidian walked out of the training ring, but Shadow couldn't help but feel nervous. Did he do well enough to pass? Did he make any mistakes? He replayed the training scenarios in his mind, analyzing every move he made. Despite his nerves, he felt a sense of accomplishment. He had trained for this moment for months and he felt prepared for his first proper mission.

As they walked toward the judges, Shadow took in his surroundings. The training facility was state-of-the-art, with holographic screens and advanced equipment. The walls were made of a shiny, metallic material that glinted in the bright lights overhead. Shadow noticed the other agents in training. Some were celebrating their success, while others looked disappointed. One dog who looked disappointed was the dog Shadow defeated in the ring. When Shadow looked at him, he glared.

"Who is that?" Shadow asked his mentor, nodding at the glaring dog.

"I think that is Henry. He looks mad though, if I were you I would ignore him. He looks mad at the results and blames you," Obsidian said.

Finally, they reached the judges' room. Shadow took a deep breath and walked in. The room was small, with a long table and several judges sitting behind it. Shadow and Obsidian stood at attention as the judges reviewed their performance. Shadow's heart was racing as he waited for the verdict. After what felt like an eternity, the head judge spoke up.

"Congratulations, Shadow. You have passed the training with flying colors. You are now officially a member of our team."

Shadow felt a surge of pride and relief wash over him. He had been shaking only moments before as he awaited the decision with anticipation. Shadow could hardly believe it. After working hard for so long, now he was official. He couldn't wait to see what kind of missions they would send him on next.

There was a moment of silence, and he turned to his friend, his mentor, Obsidian. He was told he had made it, but what about Obsidian? Shadow couldn't imagine going on a mission without his best friend... his mentor.

"You will accompany him, Obsidian, as you have formed a bond and did your duty to the Tofferis Empire training him well." Geoff looked at them, grinning. "You're ready for anything, and I hope I can count on you."

Shadow and Obsidian were relieved and proud. Their training mission was complete, and they had proved themselves worthy. They knew that their training and their bond as comrades had helped them succeed and they were ready for the next challenge... whatever that may be.

"What is our next mission?" Shadow asked.

"Meet me back at my office after the ceremony and we'll discuss it," Geoff said.

As Shadow and Obsidian approached the graduation ceremony, they saw a crowd of dogs gathered around the stage. Shadow's heart raced as he realized that these were the other dogs who had passed their training and were waiting to receive their honors. He could hardly contain his excitement as he walked up to the stage with Obsidian by his side.

Shadow could see several of his fellow trainees

breaking away from the crowd to congratulate him and Obsidian on their success.

"Great job, Shadow! You nailed it!" said a big, burly Rottweiler, giving him a hearty pat on the back.

"You too, Obsidian. You two make a great team," said a sleek, silver-coated Greyhound.

The adrenaline was pumping through Shadow's veins as he grinned from ear to ear, enjoying the praise and attention. He was a good dog. Shadow felt a sense of pride and accomplishment that he had never felt before. As more and more dogs came over to offer their congratulations, Shadow felt like he was on top of the world. The rigorous training, the hours of practice and the moments of self-doubt, it had all been worth it. Shadow knew he was ready for whatever challenges lay ahead, and he couldn't wait to see what the future held for him and Obsidian.

Shadow saw Henry walking out of the training facility, who turned his head madly at Shadow as he walked out with his mentor. He gulped, feeling sorry for the other dog.

The celebration wasn't long. They all received certificates on their completed training, had a few bowls of drinks and snacks as they were all excited about passing the rigorous training, and most of them were ecstatic to get started on their first mission right away, but it was a good time to catch up with some of the other trainees.

Until now, they had had little time for socialization since they were all training the entire time. After a bit of socialization, Shadow and Obsidian left the celebration early, eager to get started.

Excited and relieved, Shadow and Obsidian hurried back to Geoff's office. Shadow was ready to start. He didn't even want to follow the typical expectation of waiting through the night. No, he hoped to get started right away.

Shadow and Obsidian walked through the halls of the Tofferis headquarters. They took in the sights and smells of the bustling environment. They adorned the walls with motivational posters and holographic displays that showcased the latest advancements in space technology. The air was filled with the scent of fresh coffee and the hum of computers as employees rushed back and forth, tending to their duties.

As they arrived at Geoff's office, Shadow felt a mix of excitement and nervousness. This was the moment he had been working toward for months, and he wanted to make a good impression. The door to Geoff's office slid open, revealing a spacious room with a large desk in the center. They decorated the walls with awards and commendations from past missions.

As they approached the receptionist's desk, Shadow noticed a potted plant sitting in the corner, its vibrant green leaves adding a touch of life to the otherwise sterile environment.

The receptionist, a cheerful dog named Luis, greeted them with a warm smile. "Do you have an appointment?"

Shadow blinked, unsure of what to say.

"What are your names and purpose of visit?" Luis asked.

Shadow took a deep breath and introduced themselves, trying to hide the nerves in his voice. "Geoff requested we stop by his office after the ceremony."

Luis checked his computer. "Ah, yes. Geoff is expecting you." He directed them to Geoff's office at the end of the hallway.

"Thank you." Shadow grinned nervously.

They continued on their way, the anticipation building with each step. Shadow grew increasingly nervous. He was new at this, and he didn't know what they expected of him after training.

Geoff sat inside, waiting for them, a serious look on his face. "I have an important mission for the two of you." Geoff uncrossed his arms. "Our intelligence has recently uncovered a group of rogue cats that have been attacking and causing chaos on nearby planets. I need you to find and destroy any cats that cross your path."

Luis, Geoff's assistant who still stood behind them, then stepped forward and gestured toward the loading bay. "We've built a new spaceship, especially for this mission. It's equipped with the latest technology and weapons."

Luis led Shadow and Obsidian to the docking bay, where their new ship awaited them. The sleek, metallic vessel gleamed in the bright light of the bay, with its sharp lines and streamlined design making it look like they built it for speed. As they approached, Shadow could feel the excitement bubbling inside him. He had never flown a ship like this before, and he was eager to learn.

Luis gestured for them to climb aboard and opened the hatch. The smell of new technology and freshly oiled metal greeted them as they stepped inside. The interior was surprisingly spacious, with room for a small crew to live and work comfortably. Shadow ran his hand along the smooth surface of the console, taking in all the different buttons and switches, feeling the texture of the polished metal beneath his claws.

Luis showed them around, pointing out all the features of the ship. He showed them the controls for the engines, the weapons systems, and the communications array. Shadow listened intently, taking in every detail and committing it to memory. As they went through the ship, he could feel himself growing more confident and excited with each passing moment.

Finally, they arrived at the cockpit, and Luis took a seat in the pilot's chair. He gestured for Shadow and Obsidian to join him and taught them how to fly the ship.

Shadow could feel the thrill of the engines as they roared to life, the ship vibrating beneath him as they lifted off from the docking bay. Luis showed them how to steer, how to adjust the engines for speed and maneuverability, and how to fire the ship's weapons. Shadow soaked it all in, his mind racing with the possibilities of what he could do with this ship.

Geoff sent coordinates of where the rogue cats were located to their smartwatches. The little screen then flickered, and Shadow tapped his watch to turn on the live video chat.

"Coordinates have been sent. Are you two ready to depart?" Geoff asked.

Shadow scratched his ear. "Yes, sir."

"Excellent. Best of luck to the both of you, and make sure that no cats are left alive."

Luis departed the ship, and Shadow and Obsidian found themselves alone. They didn't have a crew yet. For now, it was the two of them, but they were more than capable. They could do this.

Shadow and Obsidian walked onto the bridge, each taking their positions in the cockpit. Shadow double-checked that all systems were online and functioning properly. He went through the pre-flight checklist, his heart beating faster with excitement and a hint of nervousness.

He glanced over at Obsidian, who was already at the

controls, entering the coordinates for Rhazeos. As he initiated the countdown for liftoff, Shadow could feel the vibrations from the ship's engines. He could smell the faint scent of lubricants and fuel mixed with the cool metal of the cockpit as they prepared to leave.

"Three, two, one... ignition!" Obsidian shouted, pressing down on the thruster controls.

The ship rose off the ground, and Shadow could feel the pull of the G-forces. He tightened his grip on the armrests as they left the planet's atmosphere and entered space.

The stars shone brightly all around them as they approached the designated coordinates. Shadow activated the hyper-drive, and the ship's engines roared as they shot off at light speed. The ship was now a blur of colors as they traveled faster than the speed of light.

Shadow watched the stars as they flew by, mesmerized by the colors and patterns. Obsidian remained focused on the controls, adjusting the ship's course as they navigated through the vastness of space. Shadow couldn't help but feel a sense of wonder and excitement at the unknown possibilities that awaited them on Rhazeos.

The ship jolted as it exited light speed, causing Shadow and Obsidian to grip their seats tightly. As they looked out the viewport, a stunning sight greeted them. The planet of Rhazeos loomed before them, with its swirling clouds of purple and brown, its rocky terrain, and its two bright moons orbiting around it.

Shadow couldn't help but feel a sense of awe as he gazed at the planet. It was different from any planet he had seen before, with its vibrant colors and rugged landscape. He couldn't wait to explore it, to see what secrets it held.

Obsidian was equally impressed, but he quickly regained his composure and began checking their systems. "We need to find a suitable landing spot," he said, tapping away at his console. "Somewhere that's not too heavily guarded, but still close enough to the mining facilities."

Shadow nodded in agreement and began scanning the surface of the planet for any suitable locations. As he did, he caught a whiff of something strange. It was a musty, almost metallic scent, and it made the fur on the back of his neck stand up.

"Hey, do you smell that?" he asked, turning to Obsidian.

Obsidian sniffed the air. "Yeah, that's strange. It could be a mineral deposit or something, but it's worth investigating."

With their curiosity piqued, Shadow and Obsidian plotted a course towards the source of the scent. As they approached Rhazeos, Shadow and Obsidian could see that the planet was under attack. The rogue cats maneuvered their ship through space, sparks flying off of its exterior hull, wreaking havoc. Shadow saw scraps of exterior hull floating nearby them in space. Had they already destroyed a dog ship? All Shadow saw was remains. Without hesitation, Shadow and Obsidian flew their ship into battle, determined to defend the planet and destroy the intended targets.

They fired the ship's weapons, attempting to take out the enemy ship, but the pilot was good, dodging each blast. Shadow and Obsidian worked together seamlessly, each of them knowing exactly what the other was thinking.

The enemy ship continued to evade their blasts. Shadow and Obsidian knew they needed to try something different. Shadow suggested they fly above the enemy ship and use the ship's grappling hook to latch onto it. Obsidian agreed, and they quickly put their plan into action.

Shadow expertly piloted the ship above the enemy vessel while Obsidian aimed and fired the grappling hook. It hit its target, and they were able to reel in the enemy ship, causing it to lose control and plummet towards the planet's surface.

The enemy ship crashed into the ground, causing a massive dust cloud that could be seen from miles away. Shadow and Obsidian watched from their ship as the smoke and dust cleared, feeling a sense of relief that the threat had been neutralized.

However, as they scanned the wreckage, they realized they needed to act fast. There were still enemy soldiers alive, and they could regroup if not taken care of quickly. Shadow and Obsidian quickly donned their weapons and rushed to the scene, prepared to take out the remaining enemies and finish securing the area.

stranded in the abyss

. . .

Blake

In space, no one can hear you meow!

Blake rubbed his eyes, trying to shake off the grogginess of hyperspace travel. As he looked at the screen, he realized they were not where they intended to be. He cursed under his breath, knowing that the last system they passed through had caused some damage to the StormCat. Now they were in the Rhazeos system, not exactly the best place for a cat like him.

He called out to Azalea and Fransis, his crewmates, who were still groggy from their catnaps. As they came to their senses, they saw the ship's warning lights flashing and the computer system alerting them to various malfunctions. Azalea immediately went to work on the ship's systems, trying to fix what she could. Fransis, the ship's mechanic, began checking the engines, hoping to find the source of the problem.

As they approached the planet Rhazeos, the vessel shook violently, causing Blake to lose his balance. He could feel his heart pounding in his chest as he realized the ship was going down. Azalea and Fransis were yelling out readings and warnings, trying to figure out what was happening.

Fransis worked quickly to stabilize the ship's systems, making sure they could maneuver away from the planet Rhazeos and the Tofferis Empire. But just as they thought they were in the clear, an enemy spaceship appeared out of nowhere and began attacking them.

Diego and Azalea jumped into action, manning the ship's weapons and firing back at the enemy. Blake focused on steering the ship, trying to evade the enemy's blasts and find a way to escape.

The ship lurched and shook as they attempted to outmaneuver the enemy, and Blake growled under his breath. They weren't supposed to end up here, in the middle of a battle with the Tofferis Empire. But they were fighters, and they knew they had to keep going if they wanted to survive.

Blake and his crew were caught off guard by the sudden attack. Blake tried to dodge and weave, but the enemy spaceship was fast and relentless. They fired back, but their weapons seemed to have little effect on the enemy's shields. Azalea quickly calculated the enemy's trajectory and fed the information to Blake, who maneuvered the ship to avoid a direct hit. The enemy ship fired a volley of missiles, but Fransis managed to hack into their system and redirect them back at the attacker.

"Ha! Got them!" Diego exclaimed triumphantly. But the enemy wasn't out of the game yet. They retaliated with a burst of energy that rocked Blake's ship, causing damage to the engines. The ship's alarms blared loudly, warning them of imminent danger.

"We need to get out of here!" Fransis shouted over the noise. "Engines are at 50% capacity!"

Blake knew they had to come up with a plan fast. "Azalea, see if you can hack into their system and disable their weapons."

"I'm on it!" Azalea responded, quickly typing commands into her console.

Meanwhile, Blake tried to maneuver the ship out of harm's way as they continued to exchange fire with the enemy. They were taking damage, but they couldn't afford to give up now.

"Got it!" Azalea exclaimed. "Weapons are down!"

"Alright, let's finish this," Blake said, taking control of the ship's weapons. He fired a barrage of laser blasts, hitting the enemy ship directly.

"We did it!" Fransis exclaimed, relief evident in his voice.

But their victory was short-lived as they realized the damage to the StormCat was more extensive than they thought. The engines failed, and the ship drifted aimlessly in space. They were still a long way from the CEC, and the enemy ship was still after them, though at least it was without weapons.

"Blake, light-speed is down," Fransis said urgently as he looked at the control panel. "We have to find another way out of here."

Blake looked at him, his eyes narrowing. "What do you mean, it's down?" he asked.

"I mean, it's not working," Fransis replied, his voice rising with panic as the enemy ship closed in.

Blake gritted his teeth. "Alright, we'll have to do this the hard way," he said, grabbing the controls and dodging the enemy ship's blasts.

"Enemy weapons are back online," Azalea said.

"Thanks, I never would have guessed," Blake hissed through clenched teeth.

The two ships weaved and dodged in a deadly dance through space, each trying to gain the upper hand. Blake and his crew fought with everything they had, firing every weapon at their disposal, but the enemy ship was just too powerful.

"We're not going to make it," Azalea yelled, her voice shaking with fear.

Blake looked at her, determination in his eyes. "We have to keep fighting," he said. "We can't give up now."

The enemy ship sent a missile, striking the exterior hull of the StormCat with a deafening explosion, sending shrapnel and debris flying through the air. The ship shook violently, throwing Blake, Azalea, and Fransis to the floor. Fire and smoke filled the air as warning lights and alarms blared throughout the ship.

Blake quickly scrambled to his feet and made his way to the control room, where Fransis was frantically trying to stabilize the ship. StormCat was losing power fast, and the engines were failing. Blake could feel the ship beginning to spin out of control as they hurtled toward the planet below.

"Fransis, what the meow is going on? Can you fix it?" Blake shouted over the deafening noise.

Fransis shook his head, sweat pouring down his face. "I'm trying, but the damage is too extensive. We're going down!"

Blake gritted his teeth in frustration as he tried to regain control of the ship. But it was too late. They were going to crash, and there was nothing they could do to stop it. Blake and his crew realized that they couldn't take much more damage. They needed to find a place to land before it was too late. Blake quickly scanned the area and spotted Rhazeos's moon as a potential landing site. He steered the ship toward the moon's surface, with the enemy ship hot on their trail.

The ship's controls became more difficult to manage as they descended toward the moon's surface, with warning lights flashing and alarms blaring. They braced for impact as the StormCat crashed onto the moon, metal shrieking as they tumbled to a stop.

Blake, Azalea, and Fransis quickly assessed the damage and realized they were stranded on the moon with no way to communicate for help. They gathered supplies and made a plan to survive until they could find a way off the moon and back into space.

As they looked out over the barren and desolate landscape of the moon, they realized the gravity of their situation. They were stuck on a desolate rock, with limited supplies and no way to call for help. But they refused to give up, knowing they needed to find a way to survive and escape the moon's surface.

They surveyed the damage to the ship and realized that the StormCat was beyond repair. Blake and his friends knew they had to find help and fast, as they were now stranded in an unknown hostile territory, and the Tofferis Empire would not be kind to them.

They activated their emergency beacon and hoped for the best. All they could do was wait for a rescue team or allies to find them. As they waited, they needed to keep an eye out for any signs of the Tofferis Empire, knowing that they had to be careful to not attract unwanted attention. They had to survive, repair their ship and find a way out of this mess. They didn't know what the future held for them, but they had to keep hope alive.

shadows of doubt

. . .

Shadow

In the vastness of space, even a squirrel seems like a distant dream.

Shadow looked out from his ship's window. He saw the enemy spaceship hurtling toward the moon, damaged and struggling to stay airborne. He felt a mix of emotions—relief that the enemy was taken care of, but also a sense of sadness at the destruction he was witnessing.

The ship's hull glowed red as it entered the moon's atmosphere, the friction of the air causing even more damage to the already struggling vessel. Shadow could see flames erupting from the ship's engines as it spun out of control. As it plummeted towards the moon's surface,

Shadow watched in awe as debris and smoke trailed behind the ship, creating a tail that could be seen for miles.

The crash was deafening, the sound of metal screeching and exploding echoing across the moon's barren landscape. The impact caused a shockwave that shook the ground on the surface, and Shadow felt a shiver run down his spine. As the dust cleared, he could see the wreckage of the ship scattered across the moon's surface, smoke still billowing from the twisted metal. He couldn't help but feel a sense of finality, knowing that the conflict was over, but also a sense of melancholy at the sight of so much destruction.

Shadow and Obsidian made their way toward the source of the smoke. They noticed the surrounding terrain changing from rocky outcroppings to dense forest. The trees were tall and thick, blocking out the sunlight and casting long shadows on the forest floor. Covered in moss and fallen leaves, the ground made their steps forward silent.

They neared the source of the smoke, and could hear the crackling of flames and the sound of someone moaning in pain. They quickened their pace, moving with stealth through the underbrush until they came upon a small clearing. In the center of the clearing was the wreckage of the enemy ship, still smoldering from the crash.

As they approached the crashed ship, Shadow couldn't help but feel a sense of unease. He saw a logo on the side of the ship, showing it belonged to a group of space explorers, not attackers. "Why do we have to destroy them?" Shadow tilted his head, glancing at Obsidian.

"We have to follow Geoff's orders," Obsidian replied. "He wants all cats wiped from existence."

This troubled Shadow, but he knew he had to trust in his mentor. When they reached the spacecraft, however, there was no one inside. Where had the moaning come from? Shadow scratched his ear, curious.

Obsidian saw some tracks leading away from the crashed ship and suggested they follow them. Shadow looked at the tracks and agreed, but as they followed the tracks, Shadow noticed the footprints were uneven, indicating the person who left them was limping. He also noticed that some footprints were deeper than others, suggesting the person was carrying something heavy.

Obsidian glanced at the tracks with a tilted head. He scratched his ear, then continued to study the tracks. "These tracks look too obvious." He looked from the tracks to Shadow. "I think they're trying to throw us off. I think we should go in the opposite direction."

Obsidian's words made Shadow pause and consider. He knew Obsidian was smart and had a good eye for detail, so he trusted his partner's instincts. They turned around and headed in the opposite direction, scanning the area for any signs of movement or activity.

The moon was desolate and barren, with craters and rocks as far as the eye could see. All that could be heard were the soft crunch of boots on the rocky ground and the distant hum of the crashed ship's engines. The air was cold and thin, and Shadow could feel the weight of his breathing mask on his face.

As they walked, they spotted a few small rock formations and crevices that could provide some cover. Shadow gestured to Obsidian, and they both took cover behind a large rock formation. From there, they could see the tracks they had been following, and they watched as a figure appeared in the distance, carrying a large metal box.

Shadow raised his weapon and motioned for Obsidian to stay put. He moved silently and cautiously toward the figure, his heart pounding in his chest.

Suddenly, the figure disappeared.

Shadow looked around frantically, trying to spot any sign of the individuals they were chasing. But to his dismay, they had disappeared without a trace. He scanned the area with his enhanced senses, but couldn't pick up any sounds or smells that might lead them in the right direction.

Obsidian spoke up. "I think they may have had some sort of cloaking technology. It's possible they're still nearby, but we just can't see them."

Shadow nodded. "Agreed. We need to be careful. They could be anywhere."

Shadow and Obsidian continued on their mission, searching. The weight of their decision hung heavily on their minds. They couldn't shake the feeling that they were being watched, and the unknown environment around them made them even more on edge. Shadow couldn't help but recall the propaganda they had fed him all his life about the danger and treachery of cats. They had drilled it into him since he was merely a pup, and the thought of going against it was almost unthinkable.

However, as they encountered the survivors, Shadow couldn't ignore his emotions. He saw the pain and suffering of the other beings as they attempted to escape. It was clear that these were not just enemy combatants, but living beings with their own stories and experiences. And he wondered if they were enemy combatants at all. He had seen the logo on their ship. Cat Exploration Corporation. Were they really fighters, or had Geoff fed them a lie and hoped they shot and asked questions later? The decision was a difficult one, but he knew they couldn't simply follow orders blindly without considering the implications of their actions.

Shadow continued to weigh the pros and cons, considering the potential consequences of their actions. He knew if they went against Geoff's orders, there could be severe repercussions, and they could face punishment, or even worse, if they failed in their mission. On the other hand, if they followed orders and destroyed the survivors, they would sacrifice their own morality and potentially condemning innocent beings to their deaths. It was a moral dilemma that they could not easily resolve, and Shadow struggled with the weight of the decision.

rocks and ruff decisions

. . .

Blake

In space, there's no such thing as a hairball—just zero gravity fluff!

---

*B*lake and his friends huddled together in the dark, damp cave. They were exhausted, scared, and uncertain of what was to come. Their ship had been destroyed, and they had been stranded on an unknown moon in the Rhazeos system. The sound of their breathing and the occasional drip of water from the cave's ceiling broke the silence only.

Diego spoke up first, breaking the uneasy quiet. "So, what's the plan?"

Blake, the group's leader, took a deep breath before

responding. "We need to call for backup. The diversion should hold for a while, but we can't count on it forever."

Fransis nodded in agreement. "But how are we going to call for backup? Our ship is destroyed, and we don't have any communication devices."

Azalea, who had been quiet until this point, spoke up. "I might be able to fix the emergency beacon. It's damaged, but I think I can make it work."

Fransis nodded. "And I can help her. Between the two of us, we should be able to get it up and running."

Blake turned to Diego. "We'll need your help to keep watch. Can you handle that?"

Diego nodded. "Yeah, I can do that."

They worked quickly, Azalea and Fransis tinkering with the beacon while Blake kept watch outside the cave. As they worked, they talked in hushed tones about what they would do if the Tofferis Empire found them.

"We'll fight," Fransis said, his voice steely.

Azalea shook her head. "No, we'll avoid a fight if we can. We don't stand a chance against them in a direct confrontation. Our best bet is to call for backup and hold out until they arrive."

Fransis worked on the COMM unit. His hands moved quickly and precisely over the damaged circuits. His eyes were locked onto the small screen as he tinkered with the wiring, trying to re-establish a connection. The others watched him with bated breath, knowing that their only hope for survival lay in getting a message out to their base.

Finally, after what felt like an eternity, Fransis let out a triumphant shout. "I've got it!" he exclaimed, holding up the COMM unit for all to see.

Azalea let out a sigh of relief, while Blake and Diego exchanged a look of gratitude. "Thank goodness." Blake's shoulders relaxed. "I was starting to think we were done for."

Fransis quickly set to work on the device, punching in the code to reach their base. After a few tense seconds, the screen flickered to life, and a voice crackled through the speakers.

"This is Captain Rivera," the voice crackled through. "Who am I speaking to?"

"This is Fransis, from the CEC Wonder," Fransis whispered. "We've had a bit of a situation here. We're in need of assistance."

There was a brief pause on the other end of the line before Captain Rivera's voice returned. "Understood. Please give me your coordinates, and we'll send a team out to extract you."

Fransis quickly relayed their location, while the others looked on in relief. They had done it; they had managed to contact their base and help was on the way.

Rocks crunched in the background, and Blake spun

around to see Diego skid across the ground, his hackles up, hissing.

Two black dogs entered the cave, their silhouettes loomed menacingly in the dimly lit space. Their fur was sleek and black, reflecting the dim light from outside the cave. Their muscular bodies moved with purpose, and their sharp claws clicked against the rocky surface of the cave floor. Blake and his friends crouched low, their eyes fixed on the dogs, ready to pounce or flee at a moment's notice.

Blake and his friends huddled in fear as the two dark figures emerged from the shadows. The older one stepped forward, his sharp teeth bared, and crushed the COMM unit with a single snap of his jaws. He advanced toward them, his claws glinting menacingly in the dim light.

"Please don't hurt us," Azalea pleaded, her voice trembling.

The younger one, who had been standing back, suddenly stepped forward and placed a paw on the older dog's shoulder. "Wait, we should at least hear them out before we do anything."

The older dog growled in response, but the younger one held his ground. "What harm could it do?"

Reluctantly, the older dog stepped back, and the younger one turned back to Blake and his friends. "Who are you?"

Blake took a step forward. "We're explorers."

"Explorers?" the younger dog asked.

"My name is Blake, and I am the captain. A volcano in our last system damaged some of our ship's systems, causing us to enter this system. It was not intentional."

"Lies," the older dog snapped.

"Obsidian, let's hear them out." He turned to meet Blake's eyes. "We received word that you were attacking the system."

Blake shook his head. "No. That's not true. We entered this system damaged and wanted nothing more than to leave it. However, our hyper-drive was damaged, and while we were trying to make repairs, we were attacked."

Obsidian turned to his younger dog companion. "You don't believe this nonsense, do you, Shadow?"

"I ran scans on this system, Obsidian. There were no residual laser blasts or any other traces of an attack prior to us entering this system."

"So, what do we do with them?" Obsidian asked. "We were ordered to take them out."

"They ordered us to take them out because they led us to believe they were attacking us."

"What do you suggest?"

Shadow looked from Obsidian to the cowering cats. None of them had weapons and were literally at the mercy of the two dogs. "Let's take them prisoner."

"Prisoner?"

"Geoff can decide what to do with them, but I don't see

how we can make a judgement without a full investigation."

Obsidian shook his head, growling. "We should have blasted them out of the sky. The fact that they survived doesn't bode well."

"It's the right thing to do."

Obsidian barked. "Fine. Take them prisoner... but if they resist."

Blake gulped. They had little choice but to comply.

crystal clear cat-astrophe

· · ·

Jade

In space, the laser pointer is never out of reach.

$\mathcal{J}$ade and his team boarded the shuttle and began their descent onto the massive orange planet. As they approached the planet's atmosphere, they could see the swirling clouds and the bright orange landscape. The planet seemed to be covered in a thick layer of mist and fog, making it difficult to see far ahead.

"Wow, this planet is incredible," Ryan exclaimed as he gazed out of the shuttle's window.

"Yeah, but we're not here to sightsee," Jade replied, checking the readings on his scanner. "We're here for the minerals."

The shuttle landed on the planet's surface, and the team stepped out onto the rugged terrain. The ground was a mix of rocky outcroppings and red dirt, and the air was thick with the smell of minerals.

"Okay, let's split up and start searching," Jade said, handing out mineral finders to each of his teammates. "We're looking for anything that reads high on the scanner."

As they began their search, they found small pockets of minerals scattered across the landscape. But the scanner soon led them to a large temple structure in the distance.

"Looks like the scanner is picking up something big in that temple," Jasper said, pointing to the structure in the distance.

"I have a bad feeling about this," Ryan muttered.

"Don't be ridiculous," Jade replied, leading the way toward the temple. "We came here for the minerals, and we're going to find them."

As they approached the temple, they could see that it was ancient, with large stone columns and carvings covering the walls. They made their way inside, and the mineral finder began to beep rapidly.

"There it is," Jade said, pointing to a door at the end of the chamber. "That's where the scanner is leading us."

They cautiously approached the door, which was adorned with strange symbols and carvings. Jade hesitated for a moment, but then pushed the door open.

When the door creaked open, they saw a blinding light emanating from inside the chamber. They shielded their eyes and cautiously stepped inside, drawn toward the powerful energy source.

Jade and his team crept through the temple. The air grew colder, and they felt a sense of unease. The mineral finder beeped louder as they approached the large chamber door. Ryan, the team's technician, examined the door and found that it was heavily secured.

They noticed strange markings etched on the walls. The markings resembled scratches, as if claws or sharp objects made them. Upon closer inspection, Jade realized the markings were actually a form of language, but one that he had never seen before.

Ryan, who had some expertise in ancient languages, inspected the markings. "This isn't any language that I recognize," he said, furrowing his brow in concentration. "It looks like some kind of primitive tool made it, like a claw or a rock."

Jasper, who had been scanning the temple with his handheld device, interrupted. "Guys, I'm getting some strange readings here," he said, pointing to his device. "It looks like there's some kind of energy emanating from the walls themselves."

Jade walked over to Jasper. "That's strange." He looked at the device. "There's definitely something here, but I can't quite make out what it is."

"It seems to radiate from behind this door." Jade touched a door at the end of the hallway with strange markings.

Jasper, the team's muscle, stepped forward and used his strength to force the door open. Inside the chamber, they found a glowing orb emitting a powerful energy. Jade approached the orb and scrutinized it, trying to identify its properties.

As he did so, the orb suddenly flared up with a blinding light, knocking the team off their feet. When they regained their senses, they found the orb had disappeared and the chamber was now empty.

Jade, Ryan, and Jasper looked at each other, stunned by what had just happened. They realized they had stumbled upon something beyond their understanding and knew that they needed to report their findings to their superiors. Before they could head back to their shuttle, the darkness faded once again, and the center of the room gleamed with a small object. A crystal. It flickered slightly.

Jade and his team approached the crystal. They noticed it emitting a faint glow that pulsated in a rhythmic pattern. They took out their scanning equipment to analyze the crystal and were amazed by what they discovered.

"This crystal is unlike anything I've ever seen before." Ryan studied the readings on his scanner. "It's emitting a tremendous amount of energy."

Jasper ran scans of his own. "It's also creating some sort of gravitational force field that's holding the planet in place."

Jade nodded. "That explains why this planet doesn't have any rotation. It's being held in place by this crystal."

As they continued to analyze the crystal, they noticed that its energy readings were off the charts. They speculated it could power an entire planet and provide an endless supply of energy.

"This could revolutionize the way we use energy," Jade whispered, excitement in his voice. "Imagine what this could mean for our people, for our planet."

Ryan nodded. "It's amazing, but we need to be careful with it. With this much power, it could also be incredibly dangerous in the wrong hands."

Jasper agreed. "We need to make sure that this crystal stays out of the wrong hands and that it's protected."

They carefully documented their findings and took samples of the crystal for further study. They then made their way back to their shuttle to report their discovery to their superiors.

Jade and his team boarded their spaceship. They were still in shock about what they had discovered on the orange planet. They had secured samples of the crystal and stored it safely, but they couldn't stop talking about the implications of their discovery.

"This is incredible." Jasper, the team's scientist, ran

some scans on the crystal and confirmed that it was indeed the source of the planet's stability. "If we can replicate this technology, we could stabilize other planets and prevent natural disasters caused by shifting tectonic plates."

Ryan, the team's engineer, chimed in, repeating what he'd said earlier, "but what if the technology falls into the wrong hands? It could be used as a weapon and cause catastrophic damage."

Jade nodded in agreement. "We need to get this crystal back to the MMC base on Xyrius and secure it. We also need to report our findings to the higher-ups and let them decide how to proceed."

Ryan shook his head. "We cannot just take it. We don't know what it would do to the planet. It could destabilize the entire thing. We need to bring all of our research back to the MMC and let them send an extraction team."

Jade licked his chomps. "Yes, you're right, of course. We must not leap into action. What are we, humans? No, a cat is ever patient. We'll sit back on our hind legs until we've collected all the information we need… then we'll pounce."

"I believe I need only another hour." Ryan continued entering information into his tablet, including pictures of sample data.

"Don't overlook anything. We need a thorough investigation of this crystal and its surroundings to bring back."

"Acknowledged."

Jade observed his team scan the perimeter. He helped them collect samples and data over the next hour before they loaded everything up and prepared to leave the strange planet and head back to the MMC.

Jade couldn't help but feel a sense of accomplishment as they flew toward Xyrius. They had discovered something incredible, but they also had a responsibility to ensure that it was used for the greater good.

Jade and his team landed their shuttle smoothly on the landing pad of the MMC base on Xyrius. The planet's orange sky loomed above them as they disembarked the shuttle and made their way to the main building.

Several uniformed MMC officers greeted them inside and directed them to the briefing room. The room was filled with other officers, some of whom Jade recognized from previous missions.

Jade approached one officer he knew and asked to join the briefing. The officer nodded and pointed to a table where several files and datapads were laid out.

"We've heard your report, Jade, and while this strange planet and its crystal is intriguing, I'm afraid we're not in a position to investigate it at this time."

Jade and his team listened intently as someone briefed them on the situation with some stranded cats. These were the same cats they would typically send on a mission to the planet they had briefed the MMC on. The MMC and the CEC worked together well as one explored planets and the other mined minerals from the planets. The two companies had a contract to protect each other in case of an emergency.

"Is there any way we can track them down?" Jade asked, hoping for a solution.

"We've been trying to get a signal from them, but it's been impossible. We're not sure what happened, but we think they have damaged their communication systems during a possible crash landing," the commander responded.

Ryan, one of Jade's team members, spoke up. "What about using our own communication systems to locate their distress signal? Maybe we can triangulate their position that way."

The commander nodded thoughtfully. "That's a possibility, but it won't be easy. The moon of Rhazeos is a pretty hostile environment, and the terrain is rough. It'll take some time to locate them, and we can't guarantee that they're still alive."

"Even so, how can we get onto Rhazeos' moon unseen?"

"We have a Tofferis ship."

Jade paced back and forth in the meeting room of the MMC headquarters, his tail flicking back and forth in agitation. He knew they needed to get to the planet quickly, but the idea of using a Tofferis ship made him uneasy.

"Captain, we understand your concerns," said Commander Rodriguez, one of Jade's superiors. "But this is our best option. The Tofferis ships are much faster than anything we have in our fleet, and we need to get to that planet before it's too late. Also, it can get through with little questions."

Jade sighed and ran a paw through his fur, feeling the weight of the responsibility on his shoulders. "I know, I know. It's just... the Tofferis are evil and are trying to kill us cats. It feels wrong to use their technology to help our own kind."

"But Captain, we salvaged that ship from a battle. We may be using their technology, but we are also taking it away from them. We are weakening them, not strengthening them," argued Jasper.

Jade nodded, conceding their point. "Alright, I see your point. Let's use the Tofferis ship. But we need to be careful. We don't know what kind of traps they may have left behind."

Commander Rodriguez nodded. "We'll send a team to inspect the ship and make sure it's safe for use. You and your team will depart as soon as possible."

Jade nodded, feeling the weight of the decision lift

slightly off his shoulders. "Thank you, Commander. We won't let you down."

With that, Jade and his team left the meeting room and headed for the docking bay where the Tofferis ship was waiting. Despite his reservations, Jade knew that they had a job to do, and he would do whatever it took to get it done.

rescuing whiskers

. . .

Jade

One small step for a cat, one giant leap for catkind.

---

ade, Ryan, and Jasper approached the entrance of the Tofferis solar system, where they were met by a group of guard ships. The captain of one ship hailed them.

"State your business, please," a voice came through static on the intercom.

Jasper pawed the intercom button to speak. "We're here to deliver supplies to one of the research stations on the moon of Rhazeos."

The captain narrowed his eyes suspiciously on the video screen. "I'm afraid I'll have to ask to see your face to confirm your identity."

Jasper hesitated for a moment, knowing that revealing their true identities as cats could cause trouble. Suddenly, he had an idea. He quickly hacked into the mainframe of the hologram projector on their ship and changed the image to make it appear as if they were dogs.

The captain of the guard ship studied the new image Jasper projected on his screen for a moment before nodding. "Very well. You may proceed."

After landing on the holding bay of Rhazeos, Jade, Ryan, and Jasper quickly changed into their dog disguises. They knew they had to maintain their cover if they were going to find their stranded companions on the moon.

As soon as they finished donning their disguises, Ryan grumbled under his breath. "I can't believe we're wearing these dog suits."

Jasper gave him a stern look. "Quiet down, Ryan. We need to blend in."

Jade nodded in agreement. "We can't risk drawing attention to ourselves."

As they made their way through the holding bay, they spotted an officer walking toward them.

Jade approached him cautiously. "Excuse me, officer." The dog suit muffled his voice. "We're looking for information about some cats that crashed on this moon."

The officer raised an eyebrow at them suspiciously.

"What business do dogs have with cats?" His hand hovered over his weapon.

Jasper quickly stepped in. "We were asked to question them. The Tofferis Empire wishes to find the rest of the cats, and apparently you have extracted no useful information from them as of yet."

The officer still seemed unsure, and he leaned in closer to get a better look at them. "Take off your helmets."

Jasper appeared nervous, but then he quickly tapped into the holo on his wrist and hacked into the officer's scanning device. Suddenly, their faces appeared to be those of dogs.

The officer studied them for a moment before nodding. "Alright, you can go on through. But I should warn you, we took those cats to the prison. They should have been exterminated, but for some reason, the higher-ups want them alive."

Jade's heart sank at the thought of his fellow cats being held prisoner. "Thank you for the information," he said, trying to keep his voice steady. "We'll be on our way."

Jade and company moved through the dimly-lit prison cells, their footsteps echoing through the halls. The cells were small and cramped, with barely enough room for the prisoners to move around. The air was thick with the scent of fear and desperation.

"I don't like this," Ryan muttered under his breath. "I don't think we're going to find them here."

Jade nodded, his eyes scanning the cells. "We have to keep looking. They could be anywhere."

Autumn walked up to one of the cell doors and peered inside. "It's empty." She shook her head, then looked in another cell. "This one too."

They moved further down the row of cells and heard faint sounds of movement coming from the end of the corridor. The three of them quickened their pace, the tension in the air palpable.

As Jade, Jasper, and Ryan searched the prison cells, a young dog walked up to them. "Good evening."

"Who are you?" Jade asked.

"My name is Shadow. I'm new to the field. Just finished my training." The dog paused, then tilted his head as he studied the group. "What are you guys doing here?"

Jade stepped forward and replied, "We're here to interrogate the cat prisoners that crashed on the moon."

Shadow looked them over once more. "May I see some credentials?"

Jasper quickly pulled out the forged documents they had prepared and handed them to Shadow.

After examining the papers, Shadow lowered his head and gestured in the direction of the holding cells. "They're being held over there."

Jade, Jasper, Autumn and Ryan followed Shadow's directions to a special containment cell where the four cats were being held. They cautiously approached the cell and saw the cats inside.

The cats inside of the cell began to hiss as they approached.

Jasper stepped closer to the cell bars and whispered, "we're here to rescue you."

One cat, a white American short-hair, stepped forward and cautiously sashayed toward the bars, eyeing them suspiciously. "Who are you?"

Jade stepped forward, his tail held high as he introduced himself. "I'm Captain Jade of the MMC. They've sent us to rescue you."

The cat eyed him warily, her ears flattening against her head. Jasper and Ryan stood behind Jade, their faces stern with determination.

"Why should we trust you?" the cat asked, her voice low and hesitant.

Jade understood her apprehension and took a step closer to the cell, his expression calm and reassuring. "We're all cats here, and we're all in this together. The MMC sent us to get you out of here, and that's what we're going to do. But we need your help to make it happen."

The cat looked at Jade for a moment longer before nodding her head slowly in understanding. "Alright." She glanced over her shoulder before meeting Jade's eyes once more. "What do we need to do?"

Jasper stepped forward and began working on the

lock, using his hacking skills to bypass the security system. The lock clicked open, and the cats stepped out of their cell, stretching their legs and shaking off their confinement.

"Thank goodness," she moaned in relief. "We thought we were done for."

"Thank you," another cat said gratefully, his eyes brimming with tears. "We thought we were going to die here."

Jade nodded, a solemn look on his face. "We're just doing our job." He glanced over his shoulder, back down the hallway. "Let's get out of here before anyone notices."

The cats followed them out of the cell, and they made their way back toward the holding bay, keeping a low profile and trying not to draw attention to themselves.

crystal chaos

. . .

Blake

Space travel is just like chasing a flying bug, but on a grander scale!

---

*B*lake, Azalea, Diego, and Fransis had been held captive for what felt like an eternity. They had lost track of the days, and the harsh conditions of their imprisonment had taken a toll on their bodies and spirits. But now, hope had arrived in the form of the rescue team.

As they followed the dogs through the corridors, Blake could hear chaos and commotion getting louder and louder. Suddenly, an alarm went off, blaring loudly throughout the halls. The dogs leading them broke into a run, and soon they were facing a group of dog soldiers.

"Get behind us!" one dog shouted.

Blake and his companions did as they were told. The dog soldiers charged at them, but the rescue team was ready. They fought with skill and precision, taking out the soldiers one by one.

"Come on!" the dog leading them shouted, and they continued to run toward the holding bay where the ship was waiting. The sounds of gunfire and shouting echoed through the halls, but Blake was determined to make it to safety.

The dogs protecting them were good shots, but each shot wasn't fatal. They were careful to injure only. Blake wasn't used to seeing a dog give such care, but he supposed they didn't want to harm their own.

Finally, they arrived at the holding bay, and the rescue team quickly opened the door to the ship. "Get in!" the dog leading them yelled, and they all rushed inside.

Blake and his team were relieved to be finally free, and they knew these strange dogs were to thank for their rescue. "Thank you," Blake said, looking at the dog who had led them to safety. "We wouldn't have made it without you."

The dog nodded. "We have to get out of here." He began putting his weapons and supplies away. "We can't stay here for long."

"But what about my samples?" said Fransis, a siamese cat.

"We don't have time to care about that; our lives are in danger. We must get out of here alive," Blake said.

"Lets prepare the ship for takeoff," the dog continued.

Blake and his team nodded in agreement, and they all got to work preparing the ship for takeoff. As they lifted off from the moon's surface, Blake couldn't help but feel grateful to the dogs who had saved their lives.

They had said they were part of the MMC, but how was that possible? The MMC didn't allow dogs into their ranks, not that Blake knew about, anyway. Did they have allies in the Tofferis Empire?

The Tofferis ship soared through the spaceport, its engines roaring as it raced toward the closing doors of the holding bay. Blake and his team held on tight as they braced for impact, their hearts racing with anticipation. With only seconds to spare, they managed to fly through the narrow gap; the doors slamming shut behind them.

As the ship flew away from the Tofferis solar system, Azalea let out a sigh of relief, her voice shaking slightly. "I can't believe we made it out of there alive."

Diego nodded in agreement, his eyes wide with disbelief. "Those dog soldiers were relentless."

"Not all of us are dogs," a voice interrupted. The lead dog who had rescued them was taking off his uniform, including a dog suit, to reveal himself as a cat. "I'm Jade." The rest of his dog companions took off their dog suits next. "We're all cats here. We just used disguises to get in and out undetected."

Blake and his team looked at each other in surprise. "Cats?" Fransis asked, raising an eyebrow. "I didn't expect that."

Jade chuckled. "We tried to tell you when we rescued you. The MMC is full of surprises. Now, let's get back to headquarters and report to our superiors."

The ship entered hyperspace, its engines whirring as they hurtled through the galaxy toward their destination. As they flew, Blake and his team couldn't help but feel grateful for their rescue, and impressed by the ingenuity of the cats in the MMC. They settled in for the journey ahead, eager to see what else lay in store for them.

When they arrived at the MMC headquarters, a team of officers greeted them before escorting them to a debriefing room. The atmosphere was charged with a sense of urgency and purpose. As they entered the debriefing room, the doors slid open smoothly, revealing a high-tech space adorned with holographic screens and detailed galactic maps.

Commander Rodriguez, the lead officer, gestured toward the holographic displays. "Welcome, Captain Blake and team. Please, take a seat. We have a lot to discuss." The officers arranged themselves around the room, their expressions serious but focused.

The holographic screens flickered to life, displaying

intricate details of the orange planet and its surrounding systems. "As you can see," Commander Rodriguez began, "this is the planet our scouts discovered, emitting a peculiar energy signature. Preliminary scans indicate it's unlike anything recorded in our database."

Diego leaned forward with interest. "What kind of energy are we talking about? Is it dangerous?"

Commander Rodriguez nodded. "That's what we aim to find out. The energy is fluctuating in a way that defies known patterns. Our primary objective is to investigate and determine the source. Your team has been selected for this mission due to your expertise and success in previous explorations."

Azalea raised her hand, prompting Commander Rodriguez to acknowledge her. "What kind of resistance should we expect? Any signs of potential threats?"

Officer Ian, a tactical expert, chimed in. "Our initial scans show no indications of conventional weapons or hostile forces, but we can't rule out the possibility. This mission is exploratory, but stay vigilant. Your safety is paramount."

Azalea, always the inquisitive one, asked about the specific equipment at their disposal. "What kind of tech are we bringing? Anything special for this mission?"

Commander Rodriguez provided a detailed list, outlining advanced scanners, communication devices, and personal protective gear. "You'll have the latest technology at your disposal, specifically calibrated for this mission. We want to gather as much information as possible."

The officers continued to brief Blake's team on the intricacies of the mission, discussing potential challenges and the importance of discreet reconnaissance. The conversation flowed seamlessly, with the officers sharing their knowledge and the crew absorbing every detail.

After the briefing, they were escorted to the ship that would take them to the strange orange planet Jade's team had discovered.

"Its called the Celestial Comet, since your last one was destroyed. This will be your new ship, so please do not get it destroyed too," said the officer taking them to the ship.

As they boarded the ship, Jade and his team greeted them. Jade thanked them for their help and wished them luck on their mission.

Diego spoke up. "Hey, we need a name for the planet, right?"

Blake and Azalea looked at him, and Fransis shrugged. "Sure, why not?"

Diego grinned. "Since it's powered by a crystal, let's call it Cryzatel!"

Blake and Azalea exchanged a look, then nodded in agreement. "Cryzatel it is," Blake said.

They prepared for takeoff. Blake and his team waved

goodbye to their new friends. Jade and his team returned the gesture, and the ship lifted off the ground, heading toward the mysterious planet.

The team arrived at the orange planet and made their way to the temple. The structure was ancient and ornate, with intricate carvings etched into the stone walls. As they approached the temple, they could feel the power emanating from it.

Once inside, they gazed in wonder at the enormous crystal that dominated the room. The crystal was a deep shade of orange and seemed to pulse with an inner light. Fransis approached it, his eyes gleaming with excitement.

"I can't believe we're actually here," he said, awe evident in his voice. "This is the find of a lifetime."

Blake nodded in agreement, but his expression was more somber. "We need to be careful. We don't know the full extent of the crystal's power or what effects it could have on us."

Diego stepped forward and examined the crystal, his fingers tracing its rough surface. "I think I can get a sample for research."

Blake hesitated for a moment before nodding his assent. "Be careful."

Diego produced a small instrument and carefully began chipping away at the crystal. As he worked, the others watched in tense silence. Suddenly, the planet began to tremble and shake, causing them to lose their balance.

"What's happening?" Azalea cried out, her voice filled with panic.

"It's the crystal," Fransis exclaimed, gesturing to the spot where Diego had taken the sample. "We've destabilized it!"

"You want to mention that now?" Blake screeched as they tumbled around.

The team quickly made their way to the exit, but the shaking was growing more violent by the second. They stumbled out of the temple and onto the planet's surface, watching in horror as the temple collapsed in on itself.

"We have to fix this," Blake said firmly. "We can't let this planet be destroyed."

Blake and his crew approached their ship, but as they neared, they saw strange creatures swarming around it. The bugs looked like massive crane flies, with long, spindly legs and wings that shimmered in the orange light of the planet. The crew sprang into action, rushing toward the ship and fending off the bugs with whatever they could find.

"Get them off! Get them off!" Azalea shouted as she swatted at the bugs with a piece of metal piping.

Diego continued firing his blaster, aiming for the swarm's center, where the bugs appeared to be coordinating their attack. However, the bugs' resistant exoskeletons absorbed most of the laser blasts, leaving them largely unaffected. "They're resistant to lasers!"

Despite their efforts, the bugs managed to inflict damage on the ship's hull, leaving visible scars on its once-pristine surface. Blake, realizing the urgency, shouted, "To the ship! Now!" With a swift motion, he grabbed onto the side of the ship and hoisted himself up, followed closely by his crew.

They quickly cleared the bugs off the ship, but not before some damage had already been done.

With coordinated effort, the crew fought their way to the ship's entrance. Diego, using his strength, held off a particularly aggressive group of bugs, allowing the others to board safely. As the crew members climbed aboard, Blake initiated the ship's engines.

"We need to take off now!" Fransis shouted, frantically checking the ship's systems.

The ship's thrusters roared to life, creating a gust of wind that scattered the remaining bugs. The crew, now safely aboard, witnessed the swarm dispersing beneath the ship. Blake piloted the vessel upward, leaving the swarm behind as they ascended into the planet's atmosphere.

Inside the ship, the crew caught their breath, assessing the damage. The once pristine interior now bore signs of the relentless bug attack. Blake looked at his team with determination. "We'll repair the damage and find a way to deal with those bugs. Our journey continues."

With the ship now stabilized, they set their course for the next destination, the orange glow of the planet fading in the distance.

shadows of betrayal

· · ·

Shadow

Space is just one big game of fetch with the stars.

Shadow's mind raced as he learned about the cat prisoners who broke out with the help of dogs. Was it the same group of dogs he let in earlier? Did he unknowingly contribute to their escape? Shadow relived every step, including what he remembered of the dogs. He hadn't recognized them, yet there didn't seem to be anything suspicious about them, at least none that he could recall. As he pondered this, Obsidian appeared beside him.

"Shadow, I heard what happened. It wasn't entirely your fault, but you need to be more careful in the future,"

Obsidian said, placing a reassuring paw on Shadow's shoulder.

"I know," Shadow replied, feeling a sense of guilt weigh heavily on him. "I just didn't think...I didn't know they were going to help the cats escape."

"I understand, but we need to make sure this doesn't happen again," Obsidian said firmly. "We can't risk another security breach. But don't worry, we'll keep it safe."

Shadow nodded, feeling grateful for Obsidian's understanding. "Thank you, Obsidian. I'll be more careful next time."

Obsidian gave him a small smile. "I know you will. Now, let's get back to our duties."

Shadow and Obsidian received a call on their COMM from Geoff, who requested that they come to his quarters on his ship, the Scythe. After quickly gathering their things, they boarded their own ship, the Python, and set off towards Geoff's vessel.

"I knew we should of killed the cats" Obsidian muttered as they boarded the Python.

"It wasn't the right thing to do, you know that," Shadow said.

"But at what cost, our own lives for some cats we don't even know," Obsidian growled.

As they approached the Scythe, they marveled at the sleek design of the ship. Its metallic exterior gleamed in the light of the nearby stars, and its engines hummed steadily as it hovered in space.

Once they were safely aboard, they made their way through the corridors of the ship until they arrived at Geoff's quarters. The room was dimly lit, with soft blue lights casting an otherworldly glow across the walls.

Geoff was waiting for them, sitting at a small table in the center of the room. He looked up as they entered, a small smile on his face. "Hello, Shadow, Obsidian," he said, gesturing for them to take a seat.

"I called you both here because I have some concerns," he said, his voice low and ominous.

Shadow felt a knot form in his stomach. He had a sinking feeling that this was not going to be good news.

"I have been informed that you captured some of the rebels alive," Geoff continued. "That was a mistake. You should have exterminated them, as is our protocol. Now they know too much."

Shadow and Obsidian exchanged worried glances. They had not expected this kind of reaction from Geoff. They had thought that capturing the rebels alive would be a boon for the Tofferis Empire.

"I understand, sir," Shadow said carefully. "But we thought that interrogating them might provide valuable information about their movements and plans."

Geoff snorted. "Interrogating them? You are too soft, Shadow. You don't understand how these rebels operate.

They will stop at nothing to destroy our empire. And if they get their hands on any information that could compromise us, we will all pay the price."

Shadow gulped, the hackles on the back of his neck raised.

Geoff leaned forward, his expression serious. "There's been a breach in our security protocols."

Obsidian's hackles raised as his shoulders tensed. "What kind of breach?"

Geoff hesitated for a moment before speaking. "One of our ships was stolen," he said, his voice low. "The thieves got away with sensitive information about our operations and technologies."

Shadow nodded, understanding the gravity of the situation. "What would you have us do now, sir?"

"I have a new mission for you," Geoff said, his tone clipped. "If you fail, it will be the end of you both. And possibly the end of the entire Tofferis Empire."

Shadow's teeth chattered. "What mission?"

Geoff leaned back in his chair, a thoughtful expression on his face. "I need the two of you to investigate," he said finally. "Find out who's behind this and get our information back."

"We won't let you down," Obsidian said firmly.

Geoff nodded. "I know I can count on you two," he said, a hint of relief in his voice.

Shadow and Obsidian made their way back to their

ship, the Python. As they walked, Shadow couldn't shake off the feeling of unease from their conversation with Geoff.

"I can't believe he suggested exterminating those creatures," Shadow muttered, his voice low with disgust. "It's not right."

Obsidian nodded in agreement, his expression mirroring Shadow's distaste. "I know, but Geoff has always been ruthless when it comes to protecting the Tofferis Empire's interests."

Shadow shook his head. "I don't care. It still doesn't feel right to me."

Obsidian put a reassuring hand on Shadow's shoulder. "I understand, but we have a mission to complete. We can't afford to let our emotions cloud our judgment."

With a deep breath, Shadow nodded, trying to push aside his unease. They boarded the Python and started the engines, the ship humming to life.

"So, what's our new mission?" Obsidian asked, breaking the tense silence.

Shadow pulled up the mission brief on the screen in front of him. "Weapons distribution from Lamoria."

"I thought he was having us investigate who was behind the breach?"

Shadow continued looking through the mission manifest. "It looks like we're not the lead on that, but it's a secondary mission."

Obsidian raised an eyebrow. "Well… weapons distribution then. That sounds easy enough. What's the catch?"

Shadow frowned. "The planet is in the middle of a civil war, and there are several factions fighting over control of the weapons. We need to be careful not to get caught in the crossfire."

Obsidian nodded, understanding the gravity of the situation. "We'll need to plan our approach carefully. Let's get to work."

As they plotted their course, Shadow couldn't help but think about Geoff's warning. Failure was not an option. They needed to succeed, or risk being destroyed by the Tofferis Empire.

Shadow couldn't shake off the feeling of guilt for failing to stop the rogue dogs from helping the cats escape. He knew he had made a mistake in trusting them, and it had cost the Tofferis Empire dearly. Shadow vowed to himself that he would make up for his mistake on his next mission. He couldn't afford to fail again, not after what Geoff had just told him. The thought of being destroyed for betraying the Empire sent shivers down his spine. He knew he had to focus on the mission ahead and do whatever it takes to succeed.

jade's revelation

. . .

Jade

Space is full of mysteries, just like an unopened cardboard box!

Jade sat in the cockpit of their spacecraft, a sleek vessel known as the Thunder Express, as they soared through space towards the moon of CS-78541. The mission was straightforward enough: mine korbite, a rare and valuable mineral that was in high demand among the MMC. But as they drew closer to their destination, Jade couldn't shake the feeling that something was off.

As they descended toward the moon's surface, the familiar structure of the MMC base should have been visible in the distance. But instead, Jade saw nothing but flames and smoke rising up from the wreckage. The base had been utterly destroyed.

Jade's fur bristled with a mix of fear and anger as they landed the Thunder Express near the smoldering ruins. They stepped out of the ship, their sharp senses picking up the acrid smell of burning metal and flesh. They could hear the crackle of flames and the distant sound of alarms still blaring.

Jade cautiously approached the remains of the base, careful to avoid the burning debris and twisted metal that littered the area. They saw no signs of life, no movement amidst the wreckage. It was clear that whatever had happened here had been catastrophic.

As they surveyed the scene, Jade's thoughts raced. Who could have done this? Was it an attack by a member of the Tofferis Empire, or was it an inside job? Jade's mind churned with questions as they searched for any clues that might shed light on what had happened.

Jade and the team reported to the MMC and were informed by investigators who were dispatched to the scene. Jasper suggested they try to find the source of the fire, hoping to get some clue about what had happened to the base.

They spent hours searching the debris, but found nothing that could provide a lead. Everything was burned to ash and rubble. Jade felt discouraged, as if they were running out of options.

As they continued searching, they suddenly heard the sound of a spaceship approaching. They looked up to see an MMC cruiser coming down toward their location.

Jade turned to Jasper and asked, "Do you think they found something?"

Jasper shrugged. "I don't know. Let's go find out."

The once jubilant atmosphere surrounding the crew turned somber as they witnessed the catastrophic crash of the MMC cruiser. The thunderous impact shook the ground beneath their feet, leaving an ominous trail of dark smoke rising into the air. The crew's cheers gave way to horrified gasps, their eyes fixed on the unfolding scene.

The vessel had plowed into the planet's surface, tearing through the terrain, and the echoes of its destruction reverberated through the air. Flames danced amidst the wreckage, casting an eerie glow on the surrounding area.

The crew hurriedly moved toward the crash site, a mix of dread and determination etched on their faces. As they approached, the extent of the devastation became painfully apparent. The cruiser's hull had been ripped apart on impact, leaving debris scattered across the landscape. The once sleek and formidable spacecraft now resembled a twisted metal skeleton, fragments of its outer shell strewn about like morose confetti.

Smoke billowed from ruptured sections of the ship, and sparks crackled from exposed wiring. The acrid scent of burning metal filled the air. The crew scanned the wreckage for any signs of life, their eyes searching desperately for survivors amid the chaos.

Jade, taking the lead, approached cautiously, stepping over fallen debris and avoiding patches of smoldering wreckage. The severity of the crash left little hope for the possibility of survivors, but the crew pressed on, driven by a sense of duty to their fellow comrades.

As they navigated the wreckage, they found fragments of the cruiser's infrastructure scattered across the crash site—twisted metal beams, shattered panels, and remnants of what was once a state-of-the-art spacecraft. It became increasingly clear that the impact had been brutal, leaving little chance for escape or survival.

Despite the grim scene, the crew continued their search, calling out for any signs of life amid the wreckage. The vast silence that followed their calls only intensified the weight of the moment, as the realization sank in that the once-proud cruiser had met a tragic end on the unfamiliar planet's surface.

A lone figure emerged from the twisted remains of the MMC cruiser, and as the crew focused their attention, they saw an old cat stumbling toward them.

The feline survivor bore the unmistakable signs of age —his once-sleek fur now gray and matted, his eyes clouded with the passage of time. Despite the visible toll that the crash had taken on him, the resilient cat navigated the wreckage, leaning heavily on a makeshift crutch for support.

Concern etched across their faces, the crew rushed to aid the elderly cat. With gentle hands, they guided him to a relatively stable spot amid the wreckage and offered him a canteen of water.

Jade, the leader of the crew, spoke with genuine concern. "Are you alright? Can you tell us what happened?"

Jonas, still catching his breath, nodded appreciatively. "Thank you, young ones. I'm Jonas, and I was aboard that cruiser." His voice held a timeworn yet resilient quality.

Jasper handed Jonas the water canteen, saying, "Take your time. We're here to help."

Jonas took another sip, and the crew patiently waited for him to gather himself. He began recounting his story, providing a glimpse into his past and the tragic events that led to the crash.

"I've been with the MMC for many cycles," Jonas began, his gaze distant as he recalled the memories. "We were sent to investigate the destruction of our moon base. The situation was dire, and we thought we could uncover the source of the chaos. Little did we know that it would lead to this."

He paused, the weight of his words hanging in the air.

"What happened on the moon?" Jade asked.

Jonas winced as his shoulder started to bleed again.

He applied his paw on it to relieve his wound with some pressure. Once it stopped bleeding he continued, his voice a mixture of pain and sorrow. "We found the base in ruins, attacked by an unknown force. We barely had time to react before our cruiser was targeted. I don't know who or what attacked us, but the destruction was swift and over-whelming."

As Jonas recounted the harrowing details, the crew listened in somber silence. The old cat's story painted a picture of tragedy and loss, and it became evident that the mission had taken an unexpected turn. The mysterious energy signature on the planet now held a deeper signifi-cance, intertwined with the destruction of the lunar base and the fate of Jonas's fellow crew members.

In the aftermath of the revelation, Jade spoke, his voice steady yet compassionate. "We'll do our best to uncover the truth, Jonas. You're not alone in this. We're here to help."

"We were sent here to mine some korbite," Jasper said. "Do you think that the ones that attacked wanted it?"

Jonas shook his head. "I don't know anything more," he said. "But I can help you. We can see if they stole any. I know this moon better than anyone. I can show you where to look."

The crew thanked Jonas for his help, and they radioed the MMC to inform them of the situation. They reported that they had found a survivor, and they were going to continue the investigation with his help. The MMC told them they would send out a team to pick up Jonas and take him back to the base for medical attention.

As the team returned to their ship, they couldn't help but feel a sense of unease. What had caused the destruction of the base, and the crash of the MMC cruiser? And what else lay hidden on this desolate moon?

paws and planets

* * *

Blake

Why explore the universe? Because it's there, and I'm a cat.

Blake and his friends cruised through the vastness of space, their ship gliding through the darkness. As they approached the planet Orius, they could see it in the distance, a small sphere of glowing orange light. They descended through the atmosphere, the ship's engines roaring as they burned through the thick layer of clouds.

Finally, they broke through the clouds and descended toward the surface. The landscape below was rocky and barren, with jagged mountains rising into the sky. As they approached the landing pad, they could see other ships docked nearby, their engines idling quietly.

Blake brought their ship down to the landing pad and powered down the engines. They stepped out of the ship and were greeted by the warm, dry air of Orius. The fueling station was bustling with activity, with animals of all shapes and sizes hurrying about, tending to their ships.

They made their way to the station and refueled their ship. While they waited, they took a break and explore the planet. They strolled around the station, taking in the sights and sounds of this strange new world.

After a while, they returned to their ship and checked the fuel gauge. Blake and his crew prepared to leave Orius when they heard a clanking noise coming from the storage unit of their ship. Blake and his friends cautiously approached the storage unit, trying to figure out what could be causing the clanking noise. As they slowly opened the unit, they were surprised to see a golden animal with a mane that looked like a cat, but was slightly larger than them.

"Whoa, what the catnip is that?" Diego exclaimed.

The creature turned to them and spoke in a language they didn't understand. It sounded like a mix of growls, roars, and clicks.

"What is it saying?" Blake asked, squinting his eyes in confusion.

"I don't know," Azalea replied, shaking her head.

Suddenly, the creature stopped making noises and spoke in perfect Galactic Common. "My name is Silas. I am a Lynius from the planet you call Cryzatel."

Blake and his friends were stunned. They had never encountered an alien species before.

Silas continued, "a species called Mynoras attacked my home planet. They took most of my family captive, and I was the only one who escaped. I stowed away on your ship when the Mynoras destroyed my planet."

The group looked at each other in disbelief. "What are we supposed to do with him?" one of them whispered.

Blake stepped forward. "We can't just leave him here. We have to help him."

Silas looked at Blake gratefully. "Thank you. I don't know how to repay you for your kindness."

Blake smiled. "No need to repay us. We'll help you in any way we can."

Silas, his golden fur shimmering in the soft light of the ship's interior, turned to Blake and Azalea with a warm smile. "Thank you again for rescuing me. Our home was a haven of crystal spires and lush landscapes until the Mynoras invaded."

Blake, his eyes filled with empathy, nodded. "We're sorry to hear that, Silas. But you're not alone now. We're here to help."

Azalea, always curious, chimed in. "Tell us more about Cryzatel and your people."

Silas, appreciating their interest, began to paint a vivid picture of his world. "Cryzatel was a haven of diverse ecosystems, each supported by the mystical power of the crystals that adorned our landscapes. The Lynius, my species, were the guardians of this delicate balance, ensuring the prosperity of all life."

Blake, intrigued, asked, "What happened with the Mynoras? Why did they attack your home?"

Silas's expression darkened as he recounted the painful history. "The Mynoras are a relentless species driven by conquest. They sought the power within our crystals to enhance their own abilities. We resisted, but they overwhelmed us. Many Lynius were taken captive, and our once-thriving planet was left in ruins."

Azalea, her eyes reflecting determination, stated, "Why would they do such a thing! They shouldn't get away with this. "

Encouraged by their solidarity, Silas continued, "I believe my family is still held captive by the Mynoras. With your help, we can rescue them and put an end to the threat they pose."

Blake nodded resolutely. "We're in this together, Silas. We'll find your family and stop the Mynoras."

Fransis interrupted, expressing concern about Blake's

decision to help someone they barely knew and putting them at risk.

Fransis continued, "And who knows, his family might not have survived."

Blake responded, "My dad left me and my mom died of sickness! I am not letting someone else go through the same pain as I of losing their family!"

Azalea comforted Blake by gently placing a paw on his shoulder. "Calm down, everything is fine. He didn't mean it."

Silas acknowledged any trouble caused and proposed completing the task alone if provided with a ship.

"No, it's too risky. We'll help you. We just need to return to base to let them know," Blake said.

Silas was grateful for their kindness and eagerly joined the group as they set off into space. As they traveled, Silas told them more about his planet, describing its colorful landscapes and unique creatures. The vivid images he painted with his words amazed the group.

Blake asked, "So, what exactly are Mynoras? Have you seen them before?"

Silas shook his head. "No, I've only heard stories. They are a vicious species, known for their greed and power-hungry nature. They have taken over many planets in the galaxy, enslaving the inhabitants and taking their resources. My people were no exception."

A somber mood fell over the group as they thought

about the destruction and suffering caused by the Mynoras.

"I have to find my family and stop the Mynoras from doing this to anyone else. I won't rest until they are defeated," Silas whispered.

Blake nodded in agreement. "We'll help you in any way we can, Silas. We may be just a small group, but we'll do what we can to make a difference."

With that, the group set their course for the next planet, determined to find any information or leads on the whereabouts of Silas' family and the Mynoras.

Blake and his friends marveled at the fact that they had discovered alien life. They spent hours discussing the implications of this discovery and what it could mean for the future of space exploration. Silas' presence on board added an air of excitement and wonder to their journey.

The ship they were traveling in was a sleek, silver vessel with advanced technology that allowed for long distance travel through space. It was equipped with a state-of-the-art navigation system and powerful engines that hummed quietly as they sped through the vast expanse of the cosmos.

As they made their way through the stars, they encountered all sorts of wondrous sights, from distant galaxies to beautiful nebulas. They were awestruck by the sheer size and beauty of the universe.

Despite the long journey and the repairs they had to

make to Silas' chamber, the group remained optimistic and eager to reach their destination. They knew they had a great responsibility in helping Silas find his family and stopping the Mynoras from causing any more harm.

As they finally approached the capital on the planet Caticus, they couldn't help but feel a sense of excitement and anticipation. They knew that their journey was far from over, but they were ready to face whatever challenges lay ahead.

captive in the canine abyss

. . .

Jade

They call it a black hole, but all I see is an endless abyss of possibilities!

---

*J*ade and his crew were back on their ship, still reeling from the shock of finding Jonas as the sole survivor of the MMC cruiser crash. They had tried to get him to speak about what had happened, but he remained tight-lipped and unresponsive. Jonas had said his peace when they first met him, and ever since he'd remained in his quarters, silent and reflective.

As they began to make their way back to the MMC base, their communications system beeped with an incoming message. They activated the viewscreen to see the face of an MMC officer.

"Jade, we've received word of the crash of our cruiser. We need to take Jonas back to our base for debriefing, but we currently have no room for him," the officer explained. "We request you keep him on your ship until we can make room for him."

Jade nodded in agreement. "Understood. We'll keep him with us until we reach the base."

The officer nodded back. "Thank you, Jade. We'll be in touch once we have a place for him. MMC out."

The viewscreen went dark and Jade turned to his crew. "Looks like we'll have our passenger for a little while longer," he said, a note of concern in his voice. "Let's make sure he's comfortable and well taken care of until we can hand him over to the MMC."

The crew nodded in agreement, and they all settled in for the remainder of the journey, with Jonas lying still and silent in his makeshift bed.

Jade's commander's voice crackled through the ship's communication system, "Jade, I have your next mission. I need you and your crew to head to the planet Goldera to mine some gold. We need it for our operations and Goldera is one of the few planets with an abundance of it. Understood?"

Jade replied in a respectful tone, "Yes, sir. We understand. We'll head to Goldera immediately."

The commander continued, "Be careful out there, Jade. Goldera can be a dangerous place. Keep your wits about you and return safely with the gold. The MMC is counting on you."

Jade responded confidently, "Understood, sir. We won't let you down."

With that, the communication ended and Jade and the crew set course for Goldera.

Jade and the crew traveled to the planet Goldera to complete their mission. When they arrived, they took in the planet's magnificence. The planet's surface was covered in vast golden fields, and the sight was truly breathtaking. As they began their mining operation, they couldn't help but feel a sense of awe at the abundance of wealth before them.

After several hours of hard work, they gathered a considerable amount of gold, enough to fill their storage unit and then some. Excited about their success, they made their way back to their ship, eager to return home and reap the rewards of their hard work.

The crew's triumphant cheers echoed through the metallic corridors of their ship, celebrating their successful mission on the planet Goldera. Little did they know, the shadows held a menacing secret—their once-loyal vessel had been seized by a cunning pack of dog invaders.

As the crew reveled in their victory, the ship's lights

flickered ominously. Without warning, the air crackled with the sudden appearance of a group of highly-trained dog soldiers, clad in sleek black armor, armed with laser weapons gleaming with a deadly glow.

The element of surprise was in the dogs' favor, and chaos erupted. The cats, caught off guard, hastily reached for their own laser weapons, but the dogs were quick to counter. A barrage of laser fire lit up the ship's interior, creating a chaotic dance of lethal energy.

Jade, Ryan, Jasper, and Autumn dove behind crates and control panels, returning fire as they sought cover. The pungent smell of burnt metal filled the air as laser beams scorched through the ship's surfaces.

Autumn, displaying agility and finesse, somersaulted over a barricade, firing precise shots at the advancing dogs. "We need to regroup! Fall back to the control room!" she shouted amidst the chaos.

Jade, his fur standing on end with determination, led the charge. "Hold your ground! We can't let them take our ship!"

The clash intensified as both sides engaged in a fierce firefight. Sparks flew, and the ship's alarms wailed in protest. The metallic clang of laser beams colliding resonated through the ship, creating a symphony of battle.

Jasper, exhibiting his strength, engaged in hand-to-hand combat with a formidable dog warrior. Their clashes echoed with each powerful strike, a primal dance of survival. Meanwhile, Ryan skillfully maneuvered through the chaos, hacking into the ship's systems in an attempt to turn the tide.

Amidst the turmoil, Jade and Autumn found themselves back-to-back, covering each other as they fought off the relentless assault. "We can't let them take the ship," Jade growled, determination gleaming in his eyes.

"You literally just said that," said Ryan. "We understand!"

Autumn smirked, firing a well-aimed shot. "Don't worry, Captain, not on our watch."

As the battle raged on, the cats fought with a fierce determination to reclaim their ship. The once-celebratory atmosphere had transformed into a battleground, and the outcome hung in the balance.

However, their joy was short-lived as a group of dogs who had taken over their ship suddenly ambushed them. The crew fought bravely, but the dogs were too many in number, and they were quickly overpowered as they rushed out of the control room and to the shuttle bay.

Jade and the crew quickly realized that Jonas was still inside the ship and tried to call for backup. However, their communication system was jammed and they couldn't send a distress signal. As they frantically worked to fix the comms, they heard footsteps outside the shuttle.

Suddenly, the door bursts open and a group of fierce-looking canines stormed inside. Jade and his crew fought valiantly, but they were outnumbered and outmatched. The dogs moved with ferocity and coordination, attacking the crew from all angles. Teeth and claws flashed in the dim light of the mining tunnels as the two sides clashed.

Jade drew his laser pistol and fired at the closest dog, but it dodged out of the way and lunged at him. Jade rolled to the side, narrowly avoiding the snapping jaws, and fired again. This time, his shot hit its mark, and the dog fell to the ground with a yelp.

But more dogs poured into the tunnel, their growls echoing off the walls. The crew tried to back away, but they were trapped. Jade and his crew fought with all their might, but they were quickly overpowered.

One by one, the crew fell to the relentless onslaught of the dogs. Jade fought until the bitter end, but he too was finally brought down. He lay on the ground, battered and bruised, as the dogs dragged him and his crew away to their ship.

Jade struggled to break free, but the dogs were too strong. He turned to one of them and demanded, "What do you want from us?"

The dog simply snarled in response and prodded them forward with his weapon.

They escorted jade and his crew onto the Piranha, a large, ominous-looking ship. They were led down a dimly lit corridor and into a cramped chamber. The door was locked behind them, leaving them in complete darkness. They could hear the hum of the ship's engines and the muffled sounds of the crew moving about, but otherwise, they were alone in the dark.

Jade tried to think of a way out, but his mind was foggy from the blow he had been hit with. He could barely keep his eyes open, let alone come up with a plan. They were completely at the mercy of the dog pirates now, and there seemed to be no escape.

Jade approached the guard outside their cell and asked, "What's going to happen to us?"

The dog snarled in response, "You're prisoners. We're taking you to Rhazeos. Your fate will be determined there."

Jade's ears flattened against his head as he glared at the guard. "What do you mean, 'our fate will be determined'? Are you going to execute us?"

The guard chuckled menacingly. "Maybe. Maybe not. That's for the higher-ups to decide. All I know is that you're going to Rhazeos, and you better get used to the idea of being prisoners."

Jade bared his teeth, his fur bristling with anger. "We'll never give up. We'll find a way out of here and stop you and your kind from terrorizing innocent creatures."

The guard just laughed and walked away, leaving Jade and his crew to ponder their next move.

stolen stars

· · ·

Blake

Space travel may be new to us, but I've been practicing my gravity-defying jumps for ages!

Blake, Diego, Azalea, and Fransis stood proudly in front of the Galactic Council, awaiting their reward. The Council members each wore ceremonial robes of different colors and patterns, and they all looked quite serious.

One of the Council members stepped forward and addressed the group, "Blake, Diego, Azalea, and Fransis, your discovery of Silas, a member of the Lynius species, has opened up new possibilities for intergalactic relations. The Council has decided to award you each with the

Galactic Star, the highest honor we can bestow upon those who have contributed to the advancement of our society."

The Council member handed each of them a shining medal, shaped like a star with many points. Blake held the medal up to the light, admiring its intricate design.

Diego turned to his friends and grinned. "Can you believe it? We found alien life and now we're being rewarded for it!"

Azalea nodded in agreement. "It's amazing. I never thought I'd be standing here, receiving the Galactic Star."

"It's all thanks to Silas, we wouldn't have made this discovery without him." Fransis held his head high.

The Council member spoke up again, "Your bravery and ingenuity have proven that we are not alone in the universe. May this medal serve as a reminder of your contribution to the future of our society."

The group bowed respectfully and thanked the Council before making their way out of the room, beaming with pride.

Blake and his friends returned from the ceremony. They were met with a group of scientists and security personnel surrounding Silas' chamber. The atmosphere was tense, and Blake's heart sank as he realized what was happening. Despite Blake's objections, the scientists were present to take Silas away for experimentation and testing.

The security personnel stood at attention, ready to escort Silas away at the first sign of resistance. Blake stepped forward, determined to stop them from taking his new friend. "What do you think you're doing?" he demanded, his voice shaking with anger.

One scientist stepped forward, a smug look on his face. "We are taking Silas to our labs for testing," he said. "It's for the good of science and humanity."

Blake's blood boiled at the man's words. "No," he said firmly. "You can't take him. Silas is not a lab rat. He's a living being with thoughts and feelings."

The scientist turned to him with a dismissive tone. "We have a responsibility to study any new species we come across. It's for the betterment of science and the galaxy as a whole."

Blake was outraged as the CEC scientists began to lead Silas away. "We brought him here to help him find his family, not to be experimented on!" he shouted.

The security personnel stepped forward, their hands on their weapons. "Stand down, son," one of them said. "This is not of your concern."

Blake's fists clenched at his sides as he tried to reason with them. "But he's a living being with thoughts and feelings, not just some test subject! If you do this, then we're no better than humans."

The scientists ignored his protests and continued to

lead Silas away. Blake tried to reach for him, but was restrained by security guards who had entered the room. "Let me go! You can't do this!" he shouted.

But Blake refused to back down. He stepped closer to the chamber, reaching out to touch it. Suddenly, he felt a strong hand grab his shoulder, and he was roughly pulled away. He turned to see one of the security personnel glaring at him.

"You need to leave," the guard said. "Now."

Blake felt a wave of helplessness wash over him as Silas was taken away. He could only hope that the scientists would treat him with the respect and kindness he deserved. He wanted to do something. But it was too late. Silas had been taken away, and Blake was left feeling helpless and angry at the CEC.

Blake, Diego, Azalea, and Fransis sat in the cockpit of their ship, the weight of their recent encounter heavy on their minds. As they sat in silence, Blake spoke up.

"I can't just let them experiment on Silas like that. We have to help him find his family and stop those Mynoras from destroying any more planets."

Diego looked hesitant. "We could get into a lot of trouble for stealing him, Blake."

"I know, but we can't just stand by and do nothing. We have a chance to make a difference."

Azalea nodded in agreement. "I'm in. Let's do this."

Fransis sighed, but ultimately nodded as well. "Alright, let's get Silas and get out of here."

Blake and his friends moved stealthily through the CEC base, making their way to Silas' cell. They managed to bypass several security checkpoints, but their luck ran out when a guard changing shifts caught them in the act.

"Hey, what are you doing there?" the guard yelled, reaching for her weapon.

Blake and his friends moved quickly, overpowering the guard and taking her weapon. They made a run for it, with alarms blaring and security personnel hot on their heels. They managed to make it to their ship, where they found Silas waiting for them.

"Quick, let's get out of here!" Blake yelled as they climbed aboard.

They blasted off into the atmosphere, but soon they were pursued by three CEC defense attack ships. Their ship was not meant for combat, so they swerved and dodged as best they could, but the enemy ships were relentless.

"Blake, what do we do? We can't outrun them forever!" Diego shouted.

Blake gritted his teeth, trying to come up with a plan. Suddenly, one of the enemy ships crashed into another, causing an explosion that shook their ship. The last enemy ship fired at them, but Blake was quick to respond. He spun the ship around, narrowly dodging the blast.

"Hang on, guys! We're going into hyperspace!" Blake shouted.

The ship jumped into hyperspace, leaving the pursuing ships far behind. As they emerged from hyperspace, they breathed a sigh of relief. But they knew that their troubles were far from over.

howling defiance

. . .

Shadow

Lift your leg to the moon – we're marking our territory among the stars.

Obsidian and Shadow were in the cargo bay of their ship, overseeing the distribution of weapons from the planet Lamoria. The weapons were heavy, and the dogs had to use their brute strength to lift them onto the ship.

Obsidian, a grizzled veteran of many missions, barked orders at the younger dogs, making sure they loaded the weapons in the proper places. Shadow, his second-in-command, was more relaxed, sitting on a crate and watching the proceedings with a bored expression.

As the cargo bay doors closed, Obsidian turned to

Shadow. "We failed on our last mission," he growled. "We can't afford to mess up again."

Shadow shrugged. "Relax, Obsidian. We've done this a hundred times. What could go wrong?"

In the dim glow of the Lamorian moon, the tension hung thick in the air as Obsidian and Shadow guarded the cache of weapons they had been entrusted to distribute. The night was silent, except for the occasional rustle of leaves and the distant hum of the Lamorian wildlife.

Suddenly, the tranquility shattered as a group of shadowy figures emerged from the darkness, swiftly advancing toward the duo. The moonlight revealed their feline silhouettes, and the dogs tensed, realizing they were facing an unknown group of cats. The cats moved with a calculated precision, their eyes gleaming in the moonlight with an unsettling determination.

"Stay sharp, Shadow. We don't know who they are," Obsidian whispered, his ears perked, as he tightened his grip on his blaster.

The tension escalated as the cats closed in, and the dogs stood their ground, ready to defend the precious cargo. Without warning, the cats launched a coordinated attack, their swift movements and precise strikes catching Obsidian and Shadow off guard.

Blaster fire illuminated the night as the two sides clashed in a chaotic dance. Obsidian fought with seasoned expertise, countering each move with calculated precision, while Shadow, though less experienced, displayed impressive agility as he evaded attacks.

"This has to be the CFF. No one else is as coordinated. We need to get out of here and warn Rhazeos."

"The CFF?" Shadow asked.

"Cat Freedom Fighters."

The sheer numbers of the cat intruders began to overwhelm the dogs. The felines moved with an uncanny synchronization, anticipating the dogs' every move. Despite their valiant efforts, Obsidian and Shadow found themselves gradually pushed back.

Shadow looked at Obsidian nervously. "But what about the weapons? Shouldn't we try to save them?"

Obsidian shook his head. "Our duty is to get back to Rhazeos and warn them of the attack. The weapons can be replaced, but if Rhazeos is caught off guard, it could be disastrous for our pack."

As they hurried back to their ship, they could hear the sounds of battle growing louder. Explosions rocked the ground beneath them, and Shadow stumbled as he tried to keep up with his mentor.

As they cautiously made their way through the ship, they encountered a group of cats led by a determined-looking one who looked like the leader. The two groups stared each other down, weapons at the ready.

"Hand over your weapons," the cat demanded. "We won't hurt you if you cooperate."

Obsidian laughed. "You think you can take on us dogs? You're outnumbered and outmatched."

Nevertheless, this cat and his crew remained undeterred. They charged forward, and the room erupted in a chaotic brawl. Obsidian and Shadow fought fiercely, using their powerful jaws and sharp claws to fend off the cats.

Despite their best efforts, the cat and his crew overpowered the dogs and stole the weapons. As the cats made their escape, Obsidian and Shadow lay on the ground, bruised and battered.

"We failed again," Shadow grumbled.

Obsidian just shook his head. "I guess we're not as tough as we thought we were."

Shadow and Obsidian got up from their defeat, and Obsidian turned to run away. But Shadow stopped him. "Wait, we can't just give up. We have to do something. We have to show Geoff that we can succeed."

Obsidian hesitated, but Shadow's determination convinced him. They headed for their ship. As they approached the heat of battle, they saw the CFF attacking the weapon factory, and they realized they had to act fast.

Obsidian took control of the ship, dodging incoming fire and weaving through the chaos of the battle. Shadow manned the weapons, taking aim and firing back at the CFF ships. "I got one!"

Obsidian spotted an opportunity to strike and charged straight into the heart of the CFF's formation, taking them by surprise. The enemy ships scattered, trying to avoid the oncoming attack.

"Ha! That'll show 'em!" Obsidian exclaimed, feeling a rush of adrenaline.

But Shadow noticed something in the distance, a larger ship heading toward them. "Obsidian, look out!" Shadow pointed towards the incoming vessel.

Obsidian attempted to turn the ship, but it was too late. The enemy ship rammed into them, and they spiraled out of control. "We're going down!" Obsidian yelled, struggling to regain control of the ship.

Shadow grabbed hold of a lever, and with a mighty effort, pulled them out of the dive. "Hold on, Obsidian," Shadow growled, "we're not done yet."

They headed back into the fray, determined to take down the CFF and protect their home planet. "I'm with you, Shadow," Obsidian said, feeling a newfound sense of loyalty to his apprentice.

Shadow and Obsidian quickly realized they were outnumbered and outmatched. The CFF fighter ships were fast and agile, making it difficult for the two dogs to hit their targets. "We're not going to make it," Obsidian shouted over the roar of the ship's engines.

"Don't give up now," Shadow replied, his paws firmly on the controls. "Geoff is counting on us to deliver these weapons to Rhazeos. We can't let him down."

The two dogs continued to fight back, dodging and weaving through the enemy ships. Two more ships came up from behind, flanking them on either side. Shadow twirled the ship around, firing at the two ships with all they had. But the CFF ships were too fast, and enemy fire soon hit them.

The ship spiraled out of control and crashed onto the CFF mothership. Shadow and Obsidian quickly regained their bearings and saw CFF soldiers surrounded them. They knew they had to act fast if they wanted to get out alive.

Obsidian tried to start the ship's engines, but it wouldn't budge. "We're stuck," he said, panic rising in his voice.

"Get out and push!" Shadow yelled as he jumped out of the ship, pushing it with all his might. Obsidian quickly followed suit, and together they managed to jumpstart the ship's engines.

They took off just as the CFF soldiers were closing in on them. "We made it," Obsidian exclaimed, relief evident in his voice.

"We're not out of the woods yet," Shadow said, his eyes fixed on the viewscreen. "We still have to make it to Rhazeos with these weapons."

Shadow and Obsidian arrived back at Rhazeos with

their damaged ship, and as soon as they landed, Geoff, their superior, stormed over to them.

"What the bark happened out there?!" Geoff growled at them.

"We were ambushed by the CFF. We managed to fight them off, but they flanked us and we crash-landed on their ship," Shadow explained.

Geoff's face twisted with anger. "This is unacceptable! You were supposed to deliver those weapons to our soldiers! Do you have any idea what this failure could cost us? These rebels need to be stopped. They are ruining our reputation!"

Obsidian tried to speak up. "But sir, we thought-"

"I don't want to hear any excuses," Geoff interrupted. "You two are going to report to base immediately and think about your actions. We'll decide your punishment later."

Shadow and Obsidian hung their heads in shame and followed Geoff's orders, knowing they had failed their mission and disappointed their leader.

whiskers in the void

· · ·

Blake

Space is the purrfect playground for a curious cat!

---

lake and his crew were on their way to Myturas, but as they received a transmission for help from the planet Goldera, they were conflicted about whether or not to respond. Silas and Fransis were hesitant, fearing it could be a trap from the CEC, but Blake insisted they couldn't ignore a cry for help.

"We can't just leave them there, whoever they are," Blake said firmly. "We have to go and see what's happening."

Silas shook his head. "It could be a trap, Blake. The CEC could be using Jade and his group as bait to lure us back."

Azalea interjected, "But what if it's not a trap? What if they really do need our help?"

After some deliberation, they headed to Goldera and help Jade and his group. As they approached the planet, they could see smoke and chaos in the distance.

"We're going to have to land outside the city and make our way in on foot," Blake said, his voice tense with anticipation.

Blake and the crew examined the imprints left on the surface. Azalea furrowed her brow in concern. "These imprints are from a dog ship," she announced, her voice tense. "And not just any dog ship. It's the Piranha, commanded by Captain Felix."

Diego and Fransis exchanged worried glances. "That's not good," Fransis says, his voice low. "No one's ever escaped from Felix's grasp."

"So let me get this straight," said Diego. "The dogs captured us and now they captured our friends. Can we not get a break from all this capturing?"

Azalea laughed, and said, "Well, hopefully that will be the last."

Blake nodded grimly. "We need to be careful, then. If Felix is involved, this could be a trap."

Azalea nodded in agreement. "We'll need to be extra cautious and keep our guard up. We don't know what we're walking into."

The team returned to their ship and lifted off from the planet's surface, their engines roaring as they broke through the atmosphere. Blake looked out of the window and saw the CEC ship descending toward the planet, no doubt heading to investigate the same distress signal they received.

"We have to be careful," Blake warned. "We don't know what's waiting for us out there."

"I agree," Diego nodded, his eyes fixed on the scanner, scanning for any potential threats. "But we can't just leave Jade and his group in the hands of Felix and his crew. They saved us, remember? We owe them."

Fransis, who had been quiet up until now, spoke up. "Blake, what's the plan?"

Blake thought for a moment before responding. "We need to be strategic. Azalea, can you plot a course that takes us around the planet, staying out of the CEC ship's sight, and to the coordinates of the distress signal?"

"Of course," Azalea nodded, her fingers dancing across the controls.

As they made their way toward the distress signal, Blake couldn't help but feel a sense of unease. Felix was notorious for his ruthless tactics and his cunning. If they were going to rescue Jade and his group, they would need to be prepared for anything.

"The CEC ship is trying to scan us," Fransis said.

Blake growled. "Block their scanners." He turned to look at Silas. He couldn't let the CEC get hold of him. They needed to get him back to his people. "Get us out of here."

"Yes, captain."

galactic gambit

. . .

Jade

The only thing faster than light is a dog chasing a comet.

Felix walked down the dimly lit hallway of his ship, his long tail swishing back and forth with anticipation. He had finally captured the four prisoners who had caused Geoff so much trouble. Jade, Ryan, Autumn, and Jasper were all locked up in one of the cells, looking tired and defeated.

"Well, well, well," Felix said as he approached the cell. "Look who we have here. You four caused Geoff quite the headache didn't you, but now I've got you right where I want you."

Jade stood up, trying to maintain his composure.

"What do you want from us?" he asked, his voice steady despite the fear he felt.

Felix grinned, showing off his sharp canine teeth. "I've already taken all the gold I could find on your planet, but I've got an extra bonus this time. You four are worth a lot to me, especially since you caused so much trouble last time. Geoff will be proud of me for another successful capture. Don't think we didn't figure out that you were the dogs that broke out the other cats. Or well, I was the one who figured that out. No one can play me."

Ryan stepped forward, his fists clenched. "We'll never be worth anything to you. You'll never break us."

Felix chuckled. "We'll see about that. I've got plenty of ways to make you talk. But for now, I'll leave you to lick your hairballs in your cell." With that, he turned and walked away, his tail swishing back and forth with satisfaction.

Felix, the cunning dog captain of the mighty Piranha, had successfully captured the troublesome cats - Jade, Ryan, Autumn and Jasper. He had managed to apprehend them and obtain a significant amount of gold in the process. He grinned, pleased with himself as he headed toward the planet Rhazeos to drop off his catch.

As Felix landed the Piranha, he couldn't help but feel a sense of pride in his accomplishment. He had secured a hefty amount of gold and had captured the same trouble-some prisoners that had previously escaped from his grasp. He knew that Geoff would be proud of him for his latest success.

He headed toward Geoff's headquarters, where he found the imposing figure of the dog leader himself. Geoff was a large canine with scars crisscrossing his face and an intense look in his eyes. Felix approached him confidently, the captured cats following closely behind.

"Geoff, my old friend, you won't believe what I have brought you," Felix declared with a smirk.

Geoff looked at Felix, his expression unimpressed. "What is it this time, Felix? More gold?"

Felix laughed, feeling confident. "More than that, my friend. I've managed to capture the troublesome trio who caused us so much grief last time. And not only that, but I've got a hefty amount of gold to show for it."

Geoff's eyes narrowed as he examined the prisoners. "Trio? I see four prisoners before me, you mutt. Your poor counting aside, do they know the consequences of crossing us?"

Felix nodded eagerly. "Of course, Geoff. I made sure to remind them that they can't escape the wrath of Geoff."

Geoff walked up to the prisoners, his eyes boring into them. "You four thought you could escape from us?" He cackled. "You thought wrong. I have a severe punishment in mind for your actions. For now, you will rot in the cell where you rescued the cats earlier. Ironic isn't it?"

Jade, Ryan, and Jasper stood there, fear etched on their faces.

They threw Jade and his companions into the cell, and Felix watched with a satisfied smirk as the door clanged shut. Geoff then turned his attention to Shadow and Obsidian, calling them over to see what Felix had achieved.

Shadow protested, "But boss, we were so close to catching them ourselves-"

Geoff's face darkened with anger. "Silence, Shadow. You had your chance, and you blew it. Felix has done what you could not. And for your insubordination, you'll be joining your friends in the dungeon," he said, pointing to the guards to take Shadow away.

Obsidian tried to speak up in Shadow's defense, but Geoff cut him off. "You can join him too, Obsidian. I won't tolerate disobedience in my ranks," he said sternly, his gaze cold and unwavering.

Felix watched with satisfaction as the guards took away Shadow and Obsidian. He knew that Geoff's reputation for being strict was well-deserved. He couldn't wait to see what his next mission would be.

paws, claws, and galactic laws

. . .

Blake

The universe is my litter box, and I shall conquer it!

Blake and his crew, consisting of Azalea, Diego, and Fransis, had been traveling through space for days in search of the Tofferis Empire's main base on the planet Rhazeos. As they approached the planet, they noticed a small, rocky planet nearby and decided to refuel and hide their ship.

They landed on the barren planet, which was nothing more than a lifeless rock in the vast expanse of space. As they stepped out of the ship, they felt the cold and desolate air surrounding them. The planet's surface was rocky and jagged, with no signs of life anywhere.

Fransis surveyed the fueling station to ensure it was

safe from the Tofferis Empire before they continued .. to the main station

They quickly made their way to the main station and refueled their ship, making sure to restock on any necessary supplies. As they paid for their refueling, they overheard a group of travelers discussing the Tofferis Empire's recent activity on Rhazeos.

"It's a dangerous place," one of them said. "The Tofferis Empire has a stronghold there, and they've been known to be ruthless with their prisoners."

Blake nodded grimly, knowing that they were heading into a potentially dangerous situation. However, they had a job to do and they couldn't let fear hold them back.

After they finished refueling, they headed back inside of their ship to continue their journey toward Rhazeos, however on the way, Blake noticed something.

"Is that an abandoned dog ship?"

"What?" Azalea asked.

"A Tofferis Empire ship." Blake pointed.

Diego groaned. "But we just finished refueling our own ship."

"Come on." Blake motioned for them to follow.

"Wait," Fransis interjected, "Let's hide our ship so that no one can steal it like they did with this one."

"Well, you do that and meet us back here."

Blake's heart pounded as he approached the dog ship, feeling the excitement and danger of the mission ahead.

He knew hijacking and stealing a dog ship was a risky move, but it was necessary to get to the planet Rhazeos undetected. With his crew by his side, they quickly infiltrated the ship, disabling any alarms or security measures along the way.

"The fuel is full," Diego said with relief.

Blake chuckled. "Is everyone ready?"

"We have to wait for Fransis," said Azalea.

"Do we have to, though?" Diego asked.

Azalea glared at him.

"I was just kidding." He rolled his eyes.

Once Fransis returned and they had control of the ship, Blake expertly piloted it toward the entrance of the Gez system. The ship was fast and agile, making it easy for them to evade any patrols or detection systems. As they reached their destination, Blake felt a sense of relief wash over him. They had made it to Rhazeos, the location of the Tofferis Empire's main base and where many prisoners were held.

After landing on the planet's surface, Blake and his crew quickly donned their stolen dog costumes. Although they were uncomfortable and itchy, the disguises were necessary to blend in and avoid suspicion. Blake's mind was filled with possibilities as they approached the base. Would they be able to rescue the prisoners and escape undetected? Or would they be caught and face the wrath of the Tofferis Empire? Only time would tell.

Blake and his crew made their way through the winding halls of Geoff's castle. The air was thick with the smell of dog, which wasn't altogether pleasant, and Blake couldn't help but feel a sense of disgust. Dog's breath. Finally, they arrived at the section of the castle where the prisoners were being held.

They began to ask around for information on the whereabouts of the cat prisoners. It took some time, but they finally found a guard who was willing to divulge the information they needed. The guard told them that the prisoners captured from Goldera were being held in the dungeon, which was heavily guarded.

Blake knew they would have to be careful. They didn't want to cause a scene and draw unwanted attention to themselves.

Silently, they navigated the labyrinthine corridors. The dungeon's damp air clung to their fur as they approached the muffled sounds of the guards talking at the cell gate.

"How are we going to distract them?" Fransis whispered.

Blake hushed him and nodded his head to the voices of the guards.

"When is it our break?" one guard asked. "They are supposed to switch with us at one o'clock and it's two past one."

"Just relax, they're only 2 minutes late, as usual," another guard reassured him.

"I swear if they keep this up, I am going to talk to Geoff personally,"

"Work smarter, not harder," Blake whispered to Fransis.

The dungeon was damp and dark, with a musty smell that made Blake's nose twitch. Somehow, it was even worse than dog breath. They turned the corner to see the guard dogs mumbling about. They told the dogs that they were here for the next shift. The guards departed for a break, filled with relief and gratitude. Before they departed, one guard muttered that it was about time.

"Well, what do you know? It was that easy," said Azalea.

They finally reached the cell holding Jade and his crew. Azalea quietly unlocked it. Inside, they found five cats and two dogs, all of them looking worse for wear.

"Come on, we're getting you out of here," Blake whispered to the prisoners. "We're here to help."

"What about the dogs?" Diego asked.

"They're with us," Jade said.

"What do you mean they're with you?" Diego scoffed. "They're dogs. They don't even bathe themselves."

"They're not so bad. A bit too cuddly, if you ask me." Autumn licked her paw.

The two dogs were hesitant at first, but eventually, they followed Blake and his crew out of the cell and through the castle. They made their way back to the stolen dog ship, dodging guards and trying to stay unnoticed. Finally, they made it back to the ship and took off into space, leaving Geoff's castle behind them.

Blake quietly conversed with Jade about the plan and the danger they're in, quickly explaining that they need to get out before they're caught. They head toward the door, but suddenly, Felix and his soldiers appear, blocking their path.

"I knew it was you all along. Not really that smart, reusing the same costumes that were found out last time, were you?" Felix sneered. "You think you can just waltz in here? Think again!"

Blake's heart pounded in his chest as Felix gave the order to attack. Jade, Ryan, Autumn, and Jasper stood ready, poised for action. Azalea, Diego, and Fransis unsheathed their weapons, their eyes locked on Felix and his soldiers.

"Let's get out of here," Blake said, gritting his teeth. "Now!"

With that, they charged forward, weapons drawn. The sound of metal clashing against metal echoed through the dungeon as the two groups fought fiercely.

Blake fought with all his might, determined to get his friends and fellow cats out of there. He dodged blows and struck back, his muscles burning with exertion.

Just as it seemed they were making headway, a loud horn blared through the dungeon, causing Felix's soldiers to pause momentarily. It was their chance. Blake shouted for everyone to follow him as they made a mad dash toward the exit.

But as they rounded the corner, they were met with even more soldiers blocking their path. Trapped between two groups of fighters, Blake knew this was it. He drew his sword, ready to face whatever came next.

"Looks like it's the end of the line for you, Blake," Felix taunted, a sinister grin spreading across his face.

Blake's heart sank as he realized they were completely surrounded. He exchanged a quick glance with his companions, their eyes reflecting the same fear and determination he felt.

This was it - the moment they'd been dreading. As the soldiers closed in, Blake braced himself for the worst, knowing that they were in for the fight of their lives.

galactic pawsibilities

. . .

Shadow

"Exploring space is like chasing your tail—a never-ending journey."

Shadow had nearly dozed off when he had heard the creaking of the gate. His eyes had shot open as he sat up, scanning the dimly lit room for any signs of danger.

He remembered the five dogs silently approaching him, their eyes glowing with determination. The same ones who had duped him before. Shadow's instincts had kicked in as he jumped to his feet, ready to defend himself.

"Come on, we're getting you out of here," the dog whispered to the prisoners. "We're here to help."

"What about the dogs?" one of them asked.

"They're with us," Jade, the cat who Geoff had tossed them in the cell with, said.

"What do you mean they're with you?" another one of the so-called dogs asked. "They're dogs. They don't even bathe themselves."

"They're not so bad. A bit too cuddly, if you ask me," the frisky feline with them said as she licked her paw.

Shadow hesitated for a moment before nodding his head, deciding to trust them. The dogs quickly got to work, unlocking the cells of the cat prisoners and helping them out. Shadow noticed the cats were all surprised to see dogs helping them.

However, their escape was not without its challenges. As they neared the exit, they heard the sound of guards approaching. The leader of the group quickly ordered them to split up and flee in different directions. Shadow followed the group he was with and they ran as fast as they could, dodging guards and avoiding detection.

As they emerged from the prison and into the bright sunlight, Shadow turned to thank the dogs who had helped them. But before he could say anything, he heard barking coming from behind them. He turned to see Felix and his soldiers closing in on them, their weapons at the ready.

In that moment, Shadow realized that their escape was

far from over, and that their fight for freedom had only just begun.

Shadow and the cat prisoners were on the run, trying to escape Felix's grasp. They ran as fast as they could, but they knew they couldn't outrun Felix's soldiers forever.

Suddenly, Obsidian whispered in Shadow's ear, "Felix is too focused on getting the cats. We have time to escape."

Shadow nodded and they quickly made their way to their private ship.

As they took off into the sky, they breathed a sigh of relief, thinking they had escaped Felix's wrath. But they were wrong. As they flew away, they didn't realize that their ship had a safety alarm on it, set to go off if anyone other than the rightful owners tried to take it.

The ship suddenly started blaring an alarm, and Shadow cursed under his breath. "We've got to get out of here before Felix sends his soldiers after us again," he said, as he frantically tried to shut off the alarm.

But it was too late. Felix had already been alerted to their location. "Soldiers, prepare to attack!" he shouted to his troops.

Shadow and the cat prisoners were in for a fight. They knew they had to defend themselves and their freedom. They braced themselves for the coming battle, unsure if they would make it out alive.

Shadow and Obsidian quickly jumped out of the ship

and took cover behind some nearby rocks. The dog fighters were circling overhead, trying to spot them.

"We can't take them head-on," Obsidian said. "We need to find some way to outsmart them."

Shadow nodded, scanning their surroundings for any possible advantage. He spotted a cave in the distance and gestured for Obsidian to follow him.

They darted across the rocky terrain, dodging laser fire from the dog fighters. As they approached the cave, Shadow turned to Obsidian.

"Keep them distracted," he said. "I'm going to try and take them out from behind."

Obsidian nodded, pulling out his blaster and firing at the dog fighters as Shadow disappeared into the cave.

Inside, Shadow found a small cache of explosives left behind by some previous inhabitants of the moon. He quickly set up a trap at the entrance of the cave and activated the detonator.

As he sprinted back to Obsidian, the explosion rocked the cave and sent debris flying in all directions. The dog fighters were momentarily stunned, giving Shadow and Obsidian a chance to make a run for it.

They sprinted toward the nearest dog fighter, which had crash-landed a few hundred yards away. The dog pilots were scrambling to get out of the wrecked ship, but Shadow and Obsidian were upon them before they could react.

A fierce battle ensued, with blaster bolts flying in all directions. Shadow and Obsidian fought with all their might, using their dog-like agility to dodge the dog pilots' attacks.

Finally, they emerged victorious, having taken out all three dog fighters. But their ship was still destroyed, and they were stranded on the moon.

"We need to find a way off this rock," Shadow said, looking around at the desolate landscape.

Obsidian nodded. "Let's see if we can salvage anything from those dog fighters. Maybe we can cobble together some kind of transport."

They set off toward the wreckage, determined to find a way off the moon before more dog fighters arrived to hunt them down.

As Shadow and Obsidian surveyed the wreckage around them, they noticed a few salvageable parts that they could use to repair the damaged dog ship. They quickly got to work, using all the skills and knowledge they had acquired during their time as prisoners and soldiers.

"Pass me that plasma cutter," Shadow said to Obsidian as he worked on removing a piece of the wreckage that they could use to repair the wing of the dog ship. "We need to make sure this is airtight."

Obsidian nodded and handed Shadow the plasma cutter. "This should do the trick."

After several hours of hard work, they were finally able to repair the damaged ship and make it operational. However, they knew that they had to remove the tracking beacon that was installed on the ship.

"I found the tracking beacon," Obsidian said as he pulled out a small device from the dashboard. "Let me just disable it."

Shadow watched as Obsidian carefully removed the tracking beacon, making sure that they wouldn't be tracked or followed. "We need to make sure we're not followed," Shadow said. "We need to get as far away from this system as possible."

Obsidian nodded in agreement, as he crushed the tracking beacon that fell on the ground. "We need to find a safe place to lay low for a while."

With the ship repaired and the tracking beacon removed, Shadow and Obsidian took off into space, heading toward an unknown future, but one thing was for sure: they were free.

Shadow and Obsidian could finally take off in the stolen ship and leave the moon behind. They flew for hours, trying to put as much distance between them and the Tofferis Empire as possible.

As they traveled through space, Shadow couldn't help but think about everything that had happened. The battles, the escapes, the narrow brushes with death. He felt a sense of relief that it was finally over, but also a twinge of sadness that it had to end like this.

Obsidian noticed his friend's mood and placed a paw on his shoulder. "We made it out alive, Shadow," he said. "That's what matters."

Shadow nodded, but he couldn't shake the feeling that something was still wrong. Then he realized what it was. "The others," he said. "the cats and the others. They're still out there, being held captive by the Tofferis Empire. We have to go back for them."

Obsidian looked at him skeptically. "And how do you propose we do that? We're fugitives now, remember?"

Shadow thought for a moment. "We'll have to find allies. Other cats and dogs who are willing to fight against the Empire. We'll have to form a rebellion."

Obsidian disagreed. "No, I don't want to cause more trouble. I am loyal to the Tofferis empire. I will somehow get back on good terms."

Shadow shook his head as they set their course for the unknown, determined to try and get Obsidian to join his cause. As they traveled through the stars, they couldn't help but wonder what other dangers awaited them. But they were ready for whatever came their way.

about shayne price

Shayne Price is the son of Craig A. Price, and hopes to one day become a Geologist. He likes to play sports and video games. He was behind all the plot in this book. He is in the 10th grade and goes to Murphy High School.

instagram.com/sapcheeta

tiktok.com/@shayndwxjsv

pinterest.com/sap470223

about craig a. price

www.CraigAPrice.com

Craig A. Price Jr. is a USA Today bestselling author of Claymore of Calthoria Trilogy, Dragon's Call Trilogy, Dragonia Empire Series, Space Gh0st Adventures Series, and several other titles available in alternate realities. He loves to read, write, cast spells, and spend time with his beautiful wife and three children. He dreams to one day become a full-time wizard, but until then, he'll settle for being an author. With more than a dozen novels under his belt now, it's only a matter of time before he settles for world domination, but until then, you can follow his author journey as he takes over one reader's soul at a time.

Craig lives on the Alabama Gulf Coast, among the ravenous mosquitoes, humidity, and deadly predators. If you spot him in the wild, he can be dangerous, but will often be tamed by a Mountain Dew and Reese's.

To Check out all of Craig A. Price's books, visit:

https://books2read.com/craigaprice/

Visit his website

https://www.craigaprice.com/